Poisoned by the Pier

A MOLLIE MCGHIE SAILING MYSTERY #3

ELLEN JACOBSON

Poisoned by the Pier
Copyright © 2019 by Ellen Jacobson

Print ISBN: 978-1-7321602-7-9
Digital ISBN: 978-1-7321602-6-2
Large Print ISBN: 978-1-7321602-8-6

Editor: Chris Brogden, EnglishGeek Editing

First Printing: June 2019

Published by: Ellen Jacobson
www.ellenjacobsonauthor.com

For cats everywhere who put up with wearing silly costumes

and

in memory of my father-in-law who never met a rutabaga he didn't like.

CONTENTS

CHAPTER 1
DUMPSTER DIVING

What would you do if your husband announced that he had signed the two of you up for a strict diet program and tossed all your chocolate, cookies, potato chips—even your red wine—into the trash? Would you:

(a) feel his forehead to see if he had a fever;

(b) search your purse to make sure he hadn't thrown out your emergency supply of M&M'S;

(c) start to think living on a dilapidated sailboat wasn't the craziest idea he'd ever had; or

(d) go dumpster diving?

I began with (a)—checking his forehead. The only rational explanation for Scooter's behavior was that he was ill. Seriously, we're talking about a man who's addicted to sugary cereal and steals french fries off my plate. He wouldn't last a minute without regular infusions of junk food.

After determining that he wasn't sick, at least not physically (although thinking a detox was a good idea made me wonder about his mental health), I opted for (b)—rooting through my purse. Thankfully, he hadn't found my stash of M&M'S. I was definitely going to need them to deal with this crazy food regimen of his.

While I munched on my candy, I reflected on (c)—all the other harebrained schemes my husband had come up with over the years. Of course, presenting me with a sailboat named

Marjorie Jane on our tenth wedding anniversary and thinking I'd be happy about it topped the list. But this ridiculous diet was coming in a strong second.

Just think about it for a minute—what's the first part of the word "diet"? *Die*. Would you really want to go on a "die-it"? I'd much rather be on a "live-it." And living for me involved all the things Scooter had chucked in the trash—chocolate, potato chips, cookies, and wine.

After I finished the last M&M, I looked around my home and sighed. You would have sighed too if you lived where I did—on a rundown sailboat in the noisy, dusty, grimy boatyard at a marina in Florida. The yard was where repairs and maintenance were done while vessels were out of the water, their hulls supported by metal jack stands. Seeing them propped up like nautical tree houses always made me more than a little nervous, especially living in a hurricane zone. Sure, the boats were tied down with straps, but I still wondered how many would remain standing should a serious storm blow through.

We had hauled *Marjorie Jane* out of the water the previous month when we discovered a leak on board. Once she was on land, we'd realized that fixing the leak was the least of our problems. The list of boat projects we needed to tackle was endless. We were in danger of becoming long-term residents of the boatyard—the type of people who spent years working on their boats and ended up running out of money and/or enthusiasm before they ever got to use their vessels.

Yeah, you're probably thinking we're crazy. I don't blame you. I think we're crazy too. Why would anyone live on a boat? Trust me, it certainly wasn't my idea. We used to have an adorable seaside cottage—the ocean views were to die for. Unfortunately, we ended up losing our sweet little place. Please don't ask me what happened. Every time I tell the story, I get teary-eyed. Chocolate was the only thing that helped me feel better, and that, at this point in time, appeared to be in seriously short supply.

After the cottage fiasco, we had sublet a place at the Tropical Breeze condos. I fell in love with the spa tub and luxury kitchen. The fact that there were a couple of fast-food places around the corner didn't hurt either. Sadly, it was a short-lived love affair, as the owners unexpectedly came back to town, leaving us homeless again.

That's when Scooter had come up with the idea of living on our sailboat as a temporary solution. I did mention that he was the king of harebrained ideas, didn't I? If not the king, at least he had a seat on the royal court.

It was downright depressing thinking about it all. I definitely needed more chocolate. It was time to enact option (d)—dumpster diving.

After carefully climbing down the ladder attached to our boat, I walked over to the trash bin at the far end of the boatyard. Turns out I wasn't the only one with the same idea. Ben Moretti, one of our friends who lived at the marina and made ends meet by working in the boatyard, was standing next to the dumpster holding a very familiar-looking bottle of wine and a bag of Hershey's Kisses.

"Look what I found, Mollie! Major score, don't you think?" he said, grinning from ear to ear. He pointed at the plastic garbage bag by his feet. "There's even more good stuff in there. Come on, I'll share with you. What should we celebrate? That you're finished painting the bottom of your boat?"

I thought about saying we should celebrate the fact that he had rescued my vino and candy before I had to dig through the trash personally, but I didn't want to admit to him that I'd been so desperate for chocolate that I'd been about to resort to dumpster diving myself. So, I did what anyone would do in that situation—told an itty-bitty white lie.

"You don't really think I'd eat something that came from the garbage, do you?"

The young man kicked at the ground. "Well, beggars can't be choosers. Things are a little tight until payday."

I bit my lip. "I'm sorry. I shouldn't have said that."

He shrugged. "It's okay. Besides, I figure it's like the ten-second rule." I stared at him blankly. "You know how when you drop something on the floor, if you pick it up within ten seconds, it's okay to eat? I figure when it comes to fishing something out of the garbage, it's more like a ten-minute rule. And I saw Scooter toss this in here just a few minutes ago, so we're good."

"Food wouldn't last on our floor for even a second," I said. "Mrs. Moto would pounce on it and gobble it down in no time." I smiled at the thought of our Japanese bobtail cat's love of human food. Well, most human food. She did turn her nose up at asparagus. But then again, so did I.

Ben popped a Hershey's Kiss in his mouth. "Sure you don't want one?"

I refused his offer. I know, you must be in awe of my willpower. I was even impressed...for exactly five seconds. Then I grabbed the bag from him and unwrapped the chocolate morsels as quickly as I could. The bag seemed clean—no dirt or stains on it. Maybe there was something to Ben's ten-minute dumpster rule after all.

After a few more Kisses, Ben glanced

at the garbage bag, then looked at me before it slowly dawned on him. "Hey, wait a minute. If Scooter threw this out, isn't this your food?"

I sighed. "Yep, it's mine. See that bag of chips right there? They're delicious with some sour cream dip."

"Why did he throw it out?"

"He's got this crazy idea that we should go on a diet."

Ben frowned. "Why? Scooter doesn't really have a beer belly, and you look pretty good for a middle-aged woman."

"Gee, thanks," I said, popping another piece of chocolate in my mouth. "It must be my frizzy hair. People are so entranced by the rat's nest on my head they don't notice the laugh lines by my mouth and the crow's feet around my eyes."

"Your hair looks fine to me." Considering Ben's hair was pulled back in a greasy ponytail, I took this compliment with a grain of salt. He stood and wiped his hands on his tattered khaki shorts, adding to the decorative pattern of stains he had going on. "You should take all this back with you."

"I want to, but I'm afraid Scooter will just throw it out again. I need a place to stash it temporarily until he forgets about this diet and begins eating his Cap'n Crunch cereal for breakfast again like a normal human being."

Ben's eyes grew wide. He shook his head and put his finger up to his lips in a shushing motion. I felt a pair of hands squeeze my shoulders. "What's this about Cap'n Crunch?" Scooter asked after he leaned down and gave me a quick kiss on my cheek.

"Boy, you're stealthy. I didn't hear you sneak up on me," I said. "Ben was just telling me about his favorite cereals. Doesn't a nice bowl of cereal sound good right now?"

"No, that sounds awful," he said. "All

that sugar and other processed ingredients—do you have any idea what that does to your body? Like Trixie Tremblay says, 'Live Healthy, Live Long, Live Strong.'"

"Who the heck is Trixie Tremblay?" I asked.

"Is she the lady on TV?" Ben asked. "The one who wears those brightly colored leotards and legwarmers?"

"That's the one," Scooter said. "She used to be overweight and would get out of breath walking from her car to her front door. Now, thanks to science, she's unleashed the power of rutabagas and created a meal plan designed to help everyone 'Live Healthy, Live Long, Live Strong.' These days, she's slim, powerful, and full of energy."

"Did you say 'the power of rutabagas'?" I was gobsmacked. "You realize they're just root vegetables, right?"

"Ah, but that's where science comes

in. Turns out rutabagas are more than just root vegetables. They're the secret to a healthy, long, and strong life." Scooter had a dreamy expression in his eyes. "Trixie is so inspiring!"

"What you call inspiring, I call brainwashing," I said. "Why else would you throw perfectly good food away and replace it with rutabagas?"

"She didn't brainwash me. She helped me see the truth—people who love themselves care about what they put in their bodies." He put his arm around my shoulders. "And if you love someone as I love you, then you care what they put in their bodies too. I'm really doing this for you."

I narrowed my eyes. "I know what this is really about. This is because you just turned fifty."

"Ah, so it's like a midlife crisis," Ben said. He cocked his head to one side. "But didn't Mollie tell me that buying *Marjorie Jane* was your midlife crisis?"

"Hah, that's right!" I said. "One midlife crisis per customer." I turned to Ben. "Wanna hand me that bag? I'll be taking my potato chips and chocolate back home with me."

Scooter's shoulders slumped. "Come on, my little Milk Dud. Just give it a chance. It's really important to me." He stared at me with those dark-brown puppy-dog eyes of his that I always had trouble resisting.

"Did he call you his little Milk Dud?" Ben asked.

"Yeah, it's his latest pet name for me," I said.

"There's been so many that it's hard to keep track," Ben said. "Didn't he used to call you his little sweet potato? And before that, what was it—" He tightened the ponytail at the back of his neck while he tried to remember.

"Panda bear. He called me panda bear." I glanced at my husband. "Guess you won't be able to call me Milk Dud anymore. You can hardly refer to me as a chocolate-covered caramel candy while you're on this diet. What's it called, anyway?"

"Rutamentals." Ben and I both broke out laughing. Scooter frowned. "What's so funny? It makes perfect sense. It's all about getting back to the fundamentals of healthy eating, and that begins with embracing the power of the rutabaga. Get it—'Ruta' for 'rutabagas' and 'mentals' for 'fundamentals.' Rutamentals." He wrapped his arms around my waist and gave me a squeeze. "So what do you say, my little... Actually, I'm not sure what to call you now. How about my little ruta—"

I stopped him before he could finish his thought. "Why don't you stick with Milk Dud. It sounds like there are already enough root vegetables in your life."

He shrugged. "Okay. Can you at least try Rutamentals for a week?"

"Fine, I'll give it a week." I crossed my arms and gave Scooter an appraising look. "Although, it's funny how you decided to start your new diet *after* you polished off that entire German chocolate cake I made you for your birthday."

"I love German chocolate cake," Ben said.

Scooter shook his head. "I don't really think you could have called it that. There wasn't any coconut in the frosting, and that's pretty much the hallmark of the cake."

"Coconut is gross," I said. "I did you a favor by leaving it out."

"You did *yourself* a favor." Scooter stared at me pointedly. "You wanted to help yourself to some cake too. If there had been coconut in it, you wouldn't have eaten it."

I decided I didn't like the way this conversation was going, so I steered it in another direction. "I wonder why

German chocolate cake isn't the official town cake, considering this place is called Coconut Cove."

"Oh, actually it is," Ben said. "The two of you have lived here for almost a year now—I'm surprised you didn't know that already."

I shrugged. "I'm constantly learning new things about this town. Like, did you know that if you go to Alligator Chuck's BBQ Joint on your birthday, you get free nachos?" I nudged Scooter. "Aren't you glad you weren't on your diet then? And speaking of which, I have a few terms and conditions before we start Rutamentals. First, cake is allowed. Don't forget that I've entered the cake competition at the Coconut Cove Boating Festival. So, I have to bake a cake. And not just any cake, but the winning cake. Second—"

Scooter put his finger on my lips. "Terms and conditions? You sound like a lawyer."

"That reminds me," Ben said. He fished a crumpled-up envelope out of his pocket and handed it to me. "This came for you at the marina office."

I smoothed the envelope out. "It's from a law firm," I said as I ripped it open. As I scanned the letter, my jaw dropped. "You won't believe this. Our old neighbor at the Tropical Breeze condos is threatening to file a restraining order."

"A restraining order against us?" Scooter asked incredulously.

"No, not us. Against Mrs. Moto." I handed him the letter. "How do you file a restraining order against a cat?"

Ben laughed. "Especially a cat like yours. She's always wandering around the place and jumping on people's boats."

"That's because everyone is always giving her cat treats," I said. "They love it when she comes to visit."

Scooter folded up the letter. "Everyone except this lady. I guess she didn't like it when Mrs. Moto climbed through her window and made herself at home. Let me see that envelope," he said. "Hmm. This came from Mike's firm."

"Mike Wilson, the guy who just bought that new sailboat?" I asked.

"That's the one. Hey, there's something else in this envelope." He pulled a piece of paper out, then scowled. "This is ridiculous—a bill for a cat-hair removal service."

"Want some Hershey's Kisses?" Ben asked. "That might cheer you up."

Scooter reached into the bag, then stopped himself. "No. I think I'll go back to our boat and have a Red Ruta Smoothie instead. It's designed to energize you. It's made out of radishes, radicchio, ginseng, and concentrated rutabaga extract. You guys want one?"

"Yeah, I'm going to pass," I said.

"Uh, I think I'll have to give it a miss too," Ben said. "I've got a bit of a tummy ache."

"You go on ahead. I'll be right there," I said. "I need to catch up with Ben about something."

After Scooter was out of earshot, I playfully punched Ben in the arm. "Tummy ache? Yeah, right. Faker."

Ben rubbed his stomach. "I'm not faking it. Did you see all that chocolate I ate? Not to mention I polished off the potato chips when you weren't looking."

"Lightweight," I said with a smile. "Now, listen, I need you to do me a favor and stash the rest of this stuff on your boat."

"You mean until after you're finished with the diet?"

"Huh? That doesn't make sense. I'm going to need as much wine and junk food as I can get my hands on to make it through Scooter's diet."

"And I suppose you don't want your husband to know about our little arrangement."

I carefully reached into the garbage bag, pulled out a bag of Doritos, and handed them to Ben. "Is this enough to buy your silence?"

"Throw in that Kit Kat bar, and we've got a deal."

CHAPTER 2
UNICORNS IN SPACE

"Rise and shine, my little Milk Dud," Scooter said the next morning. He gently pulled back the covers and kissed me on my forehead. I propped myself up on the pillows and yawned. "How did you sleep?" he asked as he handed me my favorite coffee mug, the one with Luke Skywalker saying, "May the froth be with you."

"Fine. But I had the weirdest dream. I had turned into a giant Persian cat with luxuriant long white hair and an adorable pink bow."

"I thought you didn't like the color pink," Scooter said.

"I don't. But it's not like I have control over my dreams. If I did, I'd be dreaming about being the United Nations ambassador to Endor and having diplomatic dinners with the Ewoks, not being a huge cat wearing a bow." I stared at the lump nestled under the covers next to me. "No offense, Mrs. Moto."

"You do realize Endor isn't real, don't you? *Star Wars* was just a movie."

"Are you sure about that?" I asked. "Sure, George Lucas has a good imagination, but come on, nobody could come up with all that unless there was some basis in reality."

"Why don't you get back to your dream," Scooter suggested.

"Okay, there I was, lying on my back and sunning myself in front of a window, when that crazy neighbor lady grabbed me and shaved all my fur off with an electric razor. By the time she was finished, I resembled one of those Sphynx cats, the bald ones. Believe me —a pink bow does not look good on wrinkly, hairless skin."

Mrs. Moto peeked out from under the covers and meowed plaintively. "Don't worry. We won't let that happen to you." She snuggled against my side while I took a sip from my mug. "Gross! What is that?" I said, spitting out a foul-tasting liquid that bore no resemblance to coffee.

Scooter sat on the edge of the bed. "Remember, you agreed yesterday to do the Rutamentals program. This is the Rise and Shine Smoothie. You drink this in the morning to stimulate your energy follicles, which primes you for a vibrant day."

"My energy follicles? Are those anything like hair follicles? Wait a minute, did I lose my hair while I was sleeping? Is that why I had that dream?" I reached up and felt my head. Nope, same old frizzy rat's nest. Phew. While I may not love my hair, I still loved having hair. "The only thing I want to stimulate are my taste buds. All I want is my regular morning mocha. Chocolate and caffeine. That's the secret to a vibrant day." I handed him back my mug. "Have you actually tried this?"

"Uh, no. I wanted to give you yours first."

"Go on, take a sip."

"No way," he said. "You spit in this one."

"Trust me, that will probably make it taste better." Scooter snorted. "Fine. Go get your own cup and try some." While Scooter went into the galley, Mrs. Moto and I snuggled back under the covers. Just as I was dozing off, I heard a gagging sound. "Are you okay?" I asked.

"I'm fine," Scooter said faintly. "It just

went down the wrong way."

"See, I told you, it tastes horrible," I said. Scooter's reply consisted of more gagging, so I crawled out of bed to investigate. I found my husband leaning against the teak cupboards clutching my second-favorite mug—the one with Princess Leia riding a unicorn in space. "You look a bit green. Kind of like the color of that dreadful Rise and Shine Smoothie. Why don't you put that down, and we'll have some normal coffee, like normal people?"

He shook his head. "No, it tastes great. I must just have a stomach bug or something. I probably caught it from Ben. I'm totally committed to Rutamentals."

"Well, if it tastes so great, have another sip."

He put the mug to his mouth, took a cautious drink and then shuddered. He gave me a forced smile. "Yum."

"Very convincing," I said. "Why don't I

let you finish that while I go to the grocery store. You threw out all the ingredients for my cake, so I'm going to have to stock up again."

"Okay, but get *just* what's required for the cake. Nothing else," he said. "I've already got everything we need for our meals this week."

Mrs. Moto jumped on the counter and butted her head against my arm. "While I'm away, you better feed this one. You know how she is when she doesn't get her breakfast on time."

Scooter scratched the feline on her head and smiled. "Wait until you see what I have for you, kitty. Trixie Tremblay has a range of pet foods too." Mrs. Moto sniffed the Princess Leia mug, then sat back on her haunches and yowled.

"Wow, you're a brave man to try to feed her anything other than Frisky Feline Ocean's Delight. Good luck with that," I said as I grabbed my shower bag and a change of clothes and darted up on deck.

* * *

After a quick shower in the communal bathrooms at the marina (yes, you heard that right: communal bathrooms— life on a sailboat isn't as glamorous as you'd think), I stopped off at the best bakery in Coconut Cove—Penelope's Sugar Shack.

The lavender brick building with its bright purple awning and colorful flower boxes had beckoned to me as I drove down Main Street. I was going to need fuel before I hit the grocery store, so I picked up an extra-large cinnamon mocha and two muffins. One of the muffins was chocolate chip, because I needed an extra dose of chocolate to get rid of the taste of the Rise and Shine Smoothie. There was only so much toothpaste could do in that department.

The other one was blueberry. I figured if Scooter asked me if I'd stuck to the diet, I could tell him how I'd had fruit for breakfast. Can you believe I came up with such a cunning plan even before I'd had coffee?

When I walked into the grocery store, I was greeted by Wanda Grossman, one of the ladies from my weekly sailing class who also lived aboard her boat at the marina. She was standing behind a food demonstration table underneath a banner that read Rejoice with Rutamentals. "Come get a free sample," she said, holding up a small paper plate.

I pointed at a life-size cutout of a woman standing next to the table. She looked like a cross between Suzanne Somers from her *Three's Company* days and Aquaman himself, Jason Momoa. Yep, just as weird as it sounded. Doubly weird when you took into account the canary-yellow legwarmers, royal-blue leotard, and purple stilettos. "Is that Trixie Tremblay?" I asked.

"Yes," Wanda gushed. "Isn't she fabulous?" She waved the plate in front of me. "This is her latest creation— fermented tofu cubes drizzled with rutabaga dressing and pickled poppy seeds. It's delicious."

The smell promised anything but delicious. I took a step back to get away from the stench and bumped into a short man dressed all in gray. Gray pants, gray short-sleeved button-up shirt, gray baseball hat, and gray sneakers. His socks were probably gray too, but I decided not to investigate too closely. Men's socks always seem to smell bad, even ten seconds out of a brand-new package. But I would have rather smelled a pair of Scooter's socks after one of his basketball matches than what Wanda was serving.

"Sorry, Alan," I said as I untangled myself from the gray-clad man's camera-bag strap. His color choice matched his personality—quiet, mild-mannered, and bland. He stared at the ground and mumbled something. "What was that?" I asked.

"Can I get a picture of you trying some of Wanda's food?" he asked softly.

"Do you mind, Mollie?" Wanda asked. "Alan agreed to do a photo shoot for the company. It would be a big help if he could get photos of people enjoying the samples."

"Sorry, I wish I could help, but I'm afraid all you'd get from me is a grimace if I had to choke that down." I pointed at a woman clad in fuchsia spandex leggings and blue legwarmers. The way she was pushing her shopping cart made me think she was going to break out into an aerobics routine at any minute. "That lady seems like a likely candidate."

After being waylaid, the woman reluctantly took the plate Wanda offered her. She slowly put the fork to her lips while Alan leaned in and snapped pictures. Her face while she chewed and swallowed was expressive to say the least, and not in a good way. For someone who dressed like a Trixie Tremblay–wannabe, she didn't seem to enjoy her food. After handing the half-finished plate back to Wanda, she murmured something about having a stomach bug, then made a rapid exit.

"I'm never going to make any commission at this rate," Wanda said with a sigh. She pointed at a stack of brochures on the table. "For every person I get to sign up for the program, I earn a little bit of money. So far, I've only been able to get a few people to give it a try."

"Let me guess. One of those people was my husband."

Wanda smiled. "Yes, he was my very first customer. He was so excited to tell you all about it. How are you enjoying it so far? You really should try this sample. It's a great recipe the two of you can add to your meal plan."

I cleared my throat. I didn't want to hurt her feelings, but I didn't want to lie either. "I already had blueberries today." There, completely truthful.

"Oh, you must have had the blueberry, rutabaga, and algae breakfast bar. Trixie says they're wonderful for muscle pain. All that climbing up and down a ladder to get on and off your boat must cause a lot of aches and pains."

"It does," I said. What I didn't say was that blueberry muffins, minus any algae, were wonderful for giving you a nutritious sugar high. And nutritious sugar highs also had a way of making you forget about any aches and pains.

When Wanda asked me what I thought about the roasted parsnip swirl in the breakfast bar, I suggested that Alan take some photos of her next to the cutout of Trixie Tremblay. Before she could continue extolling the virtues of Rutamentals, Alan pointed at where she should stand, then mumbled something.

"What was that?" Wanda asked.

"I think he said that you're very photogenic. And he's right. I've always thought your green eyes were very striking with your dark hair."

Wanda smiled and tucked some stray hairs behind her ears. "Well, at my age, it isn't dark like this naturally, but it's close to the color it was when I was younger."

Alan viewed the pictures he had taken, then quietly said, "These remind me of someone I know."

"Who's that?" she asked.

He shook his head. "I can't put my finger on it. It's something about your eyes."

"They are quite distinctive," I said. "Mrs. Moto has emerald-green eyes like yours." I turned to Alan. "Maybe that's who you're thinking of—my cat."

Alan furrowed his brow. "No, not a cat."

"Do you have a sister or a cousin in the area?" I asked. "Maybe that's who Alan knows."

Wanda's lips trembled and her eyes grew moist. "I had a sister." I reached into my purse and pulled out a packet of tissues. She took one gratefully and dabbed her eyes, taking care not to smudge her eyeliner. "Sorry. I still get so choked up every time I think about her. It happened almost twenty-five years ago, but..." Her voice trailed off. She threw the tissue in the trash and took a deep breath.

I gave her a hug. "It's okay. She was your sister. No matter how much time has passed, you're still going to miss her."

"It's not just that I miss her. It's that her death was so tragic." Her expression darkened. "All because of *him*. He betrayed her. I never forgave him. How could I after what he did to her?"

While Alan shuffled his feet and stared at the ground, I racked my brain trying to figure out what to say. I wanted to ask who *he* was and what he did to her sister, but the look on Wanda's face made me think twice about that. Instead, I asked her if she wanted me to take some brochures and pass them out at the marina.

She gave me a weak smile. "That's okay. I already put some up on the bulletin board by the office. Thanks anyway." She pulled a few containers out of a cooler and placed them on the table. "I better get more samples ready."

After saying my goodbyes, I grabbed a grocery cart. As I glanced back at Wanda chopping vegetables, I thought about how lucky Wanda was to have had a sister, even if her life had been cut short. As an only child, I had always wanted siblings. I rolled the cart down the baking aisle, tossing in flour and three kinds of sugar while thinking about whether I could forgive anyone who hurt someone close to me. Betrayal could drive people to a very dark place.

* * *

Things were not going well. And that was a serious understatement. My attempt at baking a cake for the competition had turned into a disaster. So much of a disaster that I searched through all the nooks and crannies on our boat in search of any chocolate that Scooter might have overlooked in his purge.

"Aha! I found some," I told Mrs. Moto as I plopped on the couch next to her. "It was in the engine compartment. Scooter is always so worried that he's going to electrocute himself or set something on fire that he never looks in there. I think it's going to be up to me to learn about diesel engine mechanics instead of him." The calico sniffed at the plastic storage box I was holding. "See how clever I was? I put bags of chocolate inside so they wouldn't get any oil or fuel on them." I opened the lid and pulled out a bag of miniature Reese's Peanut Butter Cups. "Sure, they might be a little melted, but they'll still taste great."

I popped a few in my mouth and sighed with pleasure. Then I looked at the remnants of my baking efforts in the galley and sighed in disappointment. Dirty dishes were piled in the sink, batter had spilled on the floor, and the trash bag had ripped, causing the contents to be strewn all over the place. There's a reason why they called cooking facilities on boats "galleys"— because they in no way, shape or form resembled a proper kitchen on land. They're not worthy of the designation of "kitchenette," let alone "kitchen."

Cooking on board a boat is no small feat. First, you have to find all the ingredients. Unfortunately, they're not conveniently located in a cupboard next to your Cuisinart. You don't even have a Cuisinart. Who has room on a small sailboat for an appliance that can make your life easier? No, the bottle of vanilla you need will inevitably be squirreled away in a locker in the V-berth— otherwise known as that pointy cabin at the front of your boat—underneath spare fuel filters, bungee cords, and a life jacket. Then, once you find the vanilla, you have to put everything back. But you can't put it all back right away, because the cat has jumped inside the locker and refuses to get out.

As if locating what you need wasn't a big enough problem, counter space will make you want to tear your hair out. *Marjorie Jane*'s galley consisted of one tiny counter, and part of that counter was on top of the fridge. If you need anything out of your fridge, like butter, then you need to move everything off the counter and put it someplace else temporarily. I find that the ladder that leads up from our main cabin to the cockpit is a good place for resting things. Just make sure everyone else knows you have a bowl of cake batter sitting on one of the rungs. I won't make that mistake again.

Just thinking about it all was giving me a headache. I unwrapped another chocolate. "Hey, don't give me that look," I said to Mrs. Moto. "You have your catnip, and I have my chocolate. Let's see you give up your magical kitty-cat stress reliever. Should I dump the catnip in the trash?" She yowled. "Don't worry," I said as I stroked her head and admired the black markings around her eyes that resembled glasses, like those worn by her namesake in the old *Mr. Moto* movies. "I would never do that to you. But Scooter, now, there's someone you need to watch out for."

As she settled on my lap, I tried to figure out how I could manage to bake my cake in the tiny oven we had. It wasn't big enough to hold the special pans that one would normally use for the creation I was making. Forget about even getting a 9x13 inch pan in there, and you certainly couldn't fit two round layer pans at the same time. Not that it mattered—the latch that held the oven in place had broken. Yes, that's right, our oven swayed back and forth unless you fastened it shut. I accidentally knocked the stupid oven as I was reaching for a glass, and it rocked so much that the door swung open and the cake pan flew out onto the floor.

I had asked one of the ladies at the marina why anyone would have a crazy oven setup like that, and she told me it was for when you were out at sea. When the waves tipped your boat from side to side, the oven tilted with the motion of the boat and stayed steady. "Gimbaled" is what she told me it was called. I have another name for it, one I won't repeat here because my mother raised me right.

Goodness. See what it had come to? I had been living on a sailboat for only a short period of time and had now started to cuss like an old, crusty sailor. But at least I reserved my swearing for times when I was alone—and provoked by kitchen appliances.

Mrs. Moto batted at the crumpled-up wrappers on the sofa. One after another, she knocked them all on the floor. When I picked them up, I made the mistake of counting them. Whoa, that was a lot of chocolate. No wonder I had a bit of a tummy ache. Or maybe there really was a stomach flu going around.

After I threw the wrappers in the trash, I scraped the half-baked, half-burned cake out of the pan and into a plastic bag. "I'm going to go toss this in the dumpster," I said to my little calico fur ball. "You be a good girl and hold down the fort."

After dumping the trash, I walked back across the boatyard and spotted my friend, Penny Chadwick, the local boat broker and sailing school instructor. She was easy to pick out of any crowd—an attractive blonde always dressed head-to-toe in shades of her favorite color, pink. Today's outfit consisted of coral-colored skinny-legged jeans and a loose fuchsia blouse. I imagine she would have appreciated the pink bow I wore in my Persian cat nightmare.

Penny was standing by the sailboat next to ours, pointing out its features to a young couple. "I think you can get *Mana Kai* at a bargain price. Her current owners are quite eager to sell. Their circumstances have, um, changed, and the wife has had to move back to

Hawaii," she said with her adorable Texan twang. She caught sight of me and waved me over. "Mollie can tell you what a great boat this is. Isn't that right, sugar?"

"My idea of a great boat is one that has a dishwasher, freezer, and plenty of counter space," I said. "Oh, and room for a Cuisinart would be heaven."

Penny laughed. "Okay, maybe Mollie isn't the best person to talk to you about sailboats. They're more her husband's thing. But, admit it, you are beginning to like sailing, aren't you, sugar?" she said as she put her arm around my shoulders. "This here is my star pupil in the weekly ladies' sailing class. Here, let me introduce you. This is my client, Jeff Morgan, and his fiancée, Emily van der Byl."

As Jeff held out his hand to shake mine, I couldn't help but notice his ears. Was it my imagination, or was one considerably smaller than the other? Did people have different-sized ears? I shook my head. What a ridiculous thought—probably the result of coming down from my sugar high. It was affecting my thinking. The rest of him seemed normal. A guy in his late twenties, average height, blond crew-cut hair, and pale-blue eyes. I'm sure his ears were normal too.

Then I noticed Emily's fingers. Not because they were weirdly shaped, but because they were beautifully manicured, and because she had a gorgeous emerald ring on her left hand. She looked normal too—probably also in her late twenties, tall and slender with dark hair in a messy bun on top of her head and sporting an adorable sundress.

Jeff smiled as he saw me admiring her ring. "I surprised her with that on her birthday a few weeks ago. I know it's not a traditional engagement ring, but I love how the color matches her eyes." He put his arm around his fiancée's waist. "It's been a real whirlwind romance, hasn't it, babe?"

While he told me about the steps he had taken to keep his proposal a secret from Emily, I was entranced by his accent. He definitely wasn't from Florida. Australian, maybe? Did they have a problem with mismatched ears down under? *Stop thinking about his ears*, I told myself, which caused me to think even more about his ears. That's when I realized everyone was staring at me.

"Why are you tugging on your earlobe?" Penny asked. "Do you have an ear infection?"

I felt my face grow warm. Did they know what I had been thinking? "Uh, no," I said. "Just noticing that I forgot to put earrings on today." I turned to Emily and Jeff and smiled brightly. "Getting jewelry for a special occasion, like your birthday or an engagement, is so romantic," I said, remembering the decidedly unromantic sailboat Scooter had given me on our wedding anniversary. Fortunately, he'd redeemed himself later by giving me a lovely necklace with a diamond lighthouse pendant.

"So, what are you up to today?" Penny asked.

"I'm trying to bake a cake for the competition tomorrow. Emphasis on *trying*."

Jeff's eyes lit up. "I'm taking part too. Once we finish viewing boats, I've got to get back and finish up my entry."

Emily put her arm through Jeff's. "Wait until you see his creation. The man is a master when it comes to icing and sugar art. His cakes are so gorgeous you almost hate to eat them. Not that it stops me. Cake is my favorite dessert. If I see one, I can't help myself. I have to take a bite."

Jeff laughed. "That's why baking is

such a good hobby for me. I have an adoring fan club already built in. She has a real artistic flair—not only does she dress like a fashion plate, she also knows a beautiful cake when she sees one."

I nodded politely. Even though Jeff's cake might be artistic, mine was going to be the showstopper. Jaws were going to drop when folks got a load of my masterpiece.

"I do love fashion and cake," she said. "It drove my father to despair. He had hoped I'd have a head for accounting and go into the family business."

"What about your siblings? Can't one of them take over?"

"I'm an only child," she said with a wistful smile. "I guess you could also say I'm an orphan as well, since both of my parents have passed on. It's a good thing Jeff has a head for money. He's helping me manage my father's estate." She held out her hand and admired her ring. "I still can't believe how lucky I am."

"Oh no," Penny said, glancing toward the entrance of the boatyard. "I can't seem to get rid of him."

"Who's that?" I asked, putting my hand over my eyes to shade them from the bright sun. I saw a familiar gray-clad man walking toward us. "Do you mean Alan Simpson?"

"He's been pestering me for weeks. He wants me to hire him to take photographs of boats I have for sale. At first I humored him because he bought a sailboat from me, but then he ended up selling it a week later. He said his mom worried about him falling overboard and drowning. Lately he's been talking about getting a golf cart instead," Penny said. "I keep telling him that I'm perfectly capable of taking my own photos, but he goes on and on about how he's a professional and that if I want to be taken seriously, I should enlist his help."

"Just because some of your pictures

have been featured in a small-town newspaper doesn't make you a great photographer," Jeff said, glancing over at Alan.

"Do you know him?" Penny asked.

Jeff frowned and rubbed the back of his neck. "No, not personally. I've just seen him around town."

Penny turned to his fiancée. "What about you, Emily?"

The young woman suddenly seemed absorbed in polishing her sunglasses. "Me? Why would I know him? I'm not even from Coconut Cove."

"Where are you from?" I asked.

"Do you know Destiny Key?"

"Is that the island north of here?"

Emily nodded. "It's a great location. Close enough to the big cities on the Gulf Coast, yet remote at the same time. The only way on and off the island is by ferry, and that only runs a few times a week." She glanced in Alan's direction and exchanged a look with Jeff before putting her sunglasses back on.

"Didn't you say you had a boat to show us that's in a slip at the marina?" Jeff looked at his watch. "Maybe we should head over there now. I've got to get back and put the final touches on my cake."

Alan waved tentatively as he approached the group. Emily grabbed Jeff's hand. "Why don't we meet Penny at the marina office? I could use a cold soda before we see more boats." They hurried away before Penny could respond, giving Alan the perfect opportunity to try to convince Penny to hire him. Or at least that's what I think he was doing. His mumbling made it hard to understand what he was saying.

As I turned toward my own boat, I thought about Jeff and Emily's reaction to Alan. Although people often avoided Alan when they saw him coming—even I had thought he was a bit odd when I first met him—the young couple had said they didn't know him. If that was the case, what was up with their hasty departure?

CHAPTER 3
MINIATURE CROP CIRCLES

Thanks to a friend's generous offer to let me use her family's spacious, well-equipped kitchen, I had finally managed to finish my entry for the cake competition. I was in a great mood—my cake looked amazing, my friend had fed me pizza before I left (mercifully free of rutabaga extract), and now I was out for an evening stroll with Scooter and Mrs. Moto.

Yes, that's right. Our cat goes for walks with us on a leash just like a dog.

Oops. I probably shouldn't have compared her to a dog. She would be so insulted. Let's keep that between us, okay? If she asks, tell her we were talking about the fact that she's no ordinary cat. After all, how many cats do you know who find important clues that lead to solving murder mysteries?

As the three of us meandered along one of the pathways in the waterfront park, I pointed at a grassy area next to a clump of oak trees. "I think that's where the booth will be."

"Uh-huh," Scooter mumbled without glancing up from his phone.

"Did you hear what I said?"

"Sure…something about your tooth."

"No, not my tooth, my booth! The FAROUT booth."

He continued to stare at the screen. "Uh-huh. Your tooth is far out."

"No, not that kind of 'far out.'" I yanked the phone out of his hand. "FAROUT, as in the Federation for Alien Research,

Outreach, and UFO Tracking." I cocked my head. "You know, the organization I work for."

Sometimes, Scooter had to be reminded that I had an important job, just as important as his. He spent his days on conference calls, staring at really boring spreadsheets, and reading all sorts of technical documents. I had to stifle a yawn every time I peeked at his computer. It was possibly even more boring than watching golf on TV.

My job was far more interesting. Investigating UFO sightings, interviewing people about alien abductions, and educating the public about our extraterrestrial neighbors—now, that was fascinating work. Sure, I didn't get paid, but as the saying went, "Volunteering ain't for sissies."

Scooter tried to grab his phone back. "Enough work, already," I said, shoving it into my purse. "We're here to relax and have a good time." I squeezed his hand. "And you definitely need to relax."

"It's hard to relax when you're dealing with a contract dispute. Losing all those business records in that fire didn't help either." He held up his hand. "Don't say it."

"Say what?" I asked.

"You were going to say something about how you can't believe I run my own consulting company and deal with technology every day, yet some of my important documents weren't backed up."

"Nope, I wasn't going to say that. I was going to tell you how adorable you look with those new tortoise-shell glasses of yours."

"You realize they're the same exact frames I had before, just with stronger lenses, right?"

"Of course," I said. "I'm very observant. I noticed the stronger lenses right away."

Scooter smirked. "You noticed that my

prescription had changed from looking at the lenses?"

I shrugged. "Sure. After all, I'm an investigative reporter for FAROUT. Noticing small details is a critical part of my job. Remember how I discovered that miniature crop circle in Mrs. MacDougal's garden? Everyone else thinks crop circles have to be huge, but there are miniature ones out there. However, you have to be observant enough to notice them." I tapped my chest. "That's where I come in."

"I remember. She'll never look at her rose bushes the same way again," he said with a smile. "But I still don't think you can tell that my lenses are different." He took his glasses off, rubbed his eyes, and sighed. "Just one more sign of getting older. My eyes are getting worse. Next thing you know, I'll be wearing hearing aids." Then he patted his imaginary beer belly. "But at least I can do something about this."

I reached up and gave him a hug. "You look great to me. I'm sure Mrs. Moto would agree too." I bent down to scoop her up, but all I saw was the end of a leash without our calico attached to it. "Now where did she go?" I asked. It used to be that she'd mysteriously lose all her collars. Getting her a pretty, rhinestone-encrusted collar had put a stop to that. But lately, she had been doing a regular Houdini and getting off her leash when we weren't paying attention.

I put my hands on my hips. "If she wants to go for walks with us, she's going to have to start playing by the rules, and that means wearing her harness and her leash."

Scooter laughed. "Playing by the rules...you're hardly one to talk."

"Well, sometimes rules are stupid. Those ones you don't have to obey. But I'm worried that if Nancy sees Mrs. Moto running around loose in the park, she'll report her."

"But she lets her run around off-leash at the marina," Scooter said. "I wonder why she's never put a stop to that, considering she and Ned own the place."

"She barely tolerates that," I said. "And that's only because her grandkids love chasing Mrs. Moto around the patio area and playing hide-and-seek with her. She can't say no to them. Tell you what—let's split up and find her. You head that way," I said, pointing toward a long pier, which extended out over the water. "She could be there watching the guys fishing and hoping for a handout. I'll go over and check out the playground. You know how she enjoys going down the slide."

After searching for our elusive cat for a good quarter of an hour, I heard a voice over the loudspeaker. "Over here, my little Milk Dud!" You'd think I'd be embarrassed, but after ten years of marriage, I was used to being called some truly bizarre pet names by my husband in public. He even called me by a pet name during our wedding vows. You should have seen the minister's face.

Scooter was standing on a stage that had been set up next to the waterfront for the festival. The way he was holding the microphone and announcing my arrival reminded me of a game show host. "Here she comes, our next contestant, my little Milk Dud!" People broke out into mock applause as I neared the stage. He could be a real goofball at times. Fortunately, he was an adorable goofball.

After taking a mock bow, I noticed Mrs. Moto in the first row of folding chairs set up in front of the stage. She was cuddled up in Emily's lap and purring loudly while the young woman rubbed her belly.

Jeff was seated next to his fiancée.

"I'm not sure you're going to get your cat back," he said. "I should probably get Emily one to keep her company after we're married, given how much I travel for work."

"Or a puppy," I suggested as a terrier streaked past me, closely followed by a chocolate Labrador retriever, a German shepherd, and two Yorkies. Mrs. Moto wasn't the only one flaunting the leash laws.

"What's going on?" Scooter asked. "Nancy just kicked me off the stage."

I glanced at the impeccably dressed older woman standing behind the podium. Despite the breeze, not a strand of her hair was out of place. "Oh, yeah, I forgot to tell you. She's giving a briefing on the festival."

"Quick, let's get out of here before she sees us," he said as he scooped Mrs. Moto off Emily's lap.

"Settle down, everyone, so we can commence on time." Nancy winced at the feedback that came through the speakers. Her husband, Ned, hurried to the control panel, adjusted a few dials, and then gave her a thumbs-up. She peered over her reading glasses at everyone milling about and chatting with one another. "Take your seats," she said firmly. When she didn't get a response, she barked, "Sit!"

Scooter and I quickly planted our butts in the chairs next to Emily and Jeff. The dogs all cowered on the ground.

"Do I have to sit through this?" Scooter whispered to me. "I don't have anything to do with the festival. Why don't I meet you later?"

"It shouldn't take long," I said. "Besides, you can't get up now. Nancy would have a fit if you disturbed her presentation."

"Fine," he said, as he tried to grab my bag. "I'll just get my phone and answer a few emails."

I pulled it back. "You know better than

to go through a woman's purse. I'll get it for you." I tilted my bag so he couldn't see the package of M&M'S that his phone was nestled under. I pulled it out and handed it to him, wishing there was a way I could sneak a few chunks of chocolate into my mouth without Scooter noticing.

"Quiet down, people," Nancy said. "You don't want to get a detention slip, do you?" I wasn't entirely sure she was joking. "For those of you who don't know me, my name is Nancy Schneider. I'm the chair of the Coconut Cove Boating Festival Organizing Committee. This evening, I'm going to go through the festival schedule, explain how each event is organized, and detail the rules and regulations that everyone needs to follow."

Mrs. Moto yawned. Rules and regulations bored her. They bored me too, but I had a vested interest in two of the main events at the festival—the cake competition and the pet-costume contest—so I was paying close attention.

"The festival kicks off tomorrow," Nancy said. "It's a Saturday, so we're expecting a lot of people, including plenty of out-of-town visitors. We'll have several food booths, featuring local eateries such as the Sailor's Corner Cafe, Penelope's Sugar Shack, the Tipsy Pirate, and Alligator Chuck's BBQ Joint."

"Don't forget the Rutamentals booth," a woman cried out. I turned and saw Wanda decked out in an oversized canary-yellow T-shirt with Trixie Tremblay's smiling face emblazoned on the front. "I'll be doing cooking demonstrations and handing out free samples."

Nancy clenched her hands on the edge of the podium. "Does anyone else have anything to add?" she snapped. No one said a word, although one of the dogs whimpered. "Good. There will be a seminar on hazardous marine products led by Ned in the morning here at the main stage, followed by live music, courtesy of…" She adjusted her reading glasses and peered at the printout in her hand. "Courtesy of Eye Patches and Peg Legs."

"That's a funny name for a band, isn't it, mate?" Jeff asked Scooter.

Scooter looked up from his phone. "That's our friend Ben's band. He's a bit obsessed with pirates. They're really good. You should stick around tomorrow and watch them."

"Shush," I said. "Nancy's talking about the cake competition."

"We have seven entrants this year." As she rattled off everyone's names, I looked around and eyed up the competition—one bored teenager, identical twins named Gertrude and Gretchen, Wanda, Mike, and Jeff.

The teen seemed like she was there

under duress. How good could her cake be? You could tell when something wasn't baked with love. Rumor had it that Gretchen and Gertrude used box mixes for their cakes instead of baking from scratch. Wanda was probably going to make a Rutamentals recipe. Rutabaga-flavored cake? I couldn't imagine that would go down well with the judges. Mike was a wild card. I didn't really know much about him, other than the fact that he was a lawyer and had recently bought a sailboat. He was someone I might have to worry about. And then there was Jeff. He talked a good game, but could he deliver?

"Now, let me introduce you to the other judges who will be on the panel with me." My heart sank when I realized that Nancy was going to be one of the judges. I wasn't exactly on her good side after I had filled out the entry form in purple ink using cursive, rather than regulation black ink with block letters.

"First up is local business owner Norm Thomas," Nancy said. I put my head in my hands. There was no way I was going to win now. He had been annoyed at me ever since I'd won a bet that meant he had to rename his boat *The Codfather* to *ET*. For some reason, the silly man had objected to naming his boat after an alien who ate Reese's Pieces.

Norm grabbed the microphone from Nancy. "Glad to be here, folks. As you know, I take my responsibilities as a citizen of Coconut Cove very seriously, and what could be more important than tasting cake?" he said with a chuckle. "And as your mayor, I promise to take my responsibilities even more seriously."

"Leave it to Norm to turn a cake competition into a campaign speech," I said.

"He does realize it's only March, and the election isn't until November, right?"

Scooter asked.

I laughed. "If he had his way, he'd skip the election and proclaim himself mayor."

Nancy wrestled the microphone away from Norm. "Our next judge is Chief Dalton," she said. I groaned. I might as well give up now. The chief and I didn't exactly see eye to eye on a range of subjects, from colored markers to murder investigations. Personally, I think he felt threatened by my investigative skills. Although, maybe his extraordinarily bushy eyebrows had given him some sort of complex, which caused him to be so grumpy.

After introducing the burly man, Nancy pointed at the final judge. "We're honored to have Penelope Pringle as part of the judging panel this year. Not only is she the owner of one of Coconut Cove's most popular bakeries, the Sugar Shack, but she's also an award-winning pastry chef and was the youngest winner ever of this year's coveted Sunshine State Culinary Prize."

Penelope seemed embarrassed by Nancy's praise. "I wasn't that young, actually," she said softly into the microphone as she tucked her curly strawberry-blonde hair behind her ears.

"Trust me, dear, twenty-five is very youthful," Nancy said.

Scooter sighed. "I can barely remember when I was twenty-five. Oh, to be young again."

"Now, let me go through the details for tomorrow," Nancy continued. "Contestants must drop their cakes off at the sports pavilion by the fishing pier by nine sharp. The public will be admitted at noon to view the cakes and watch the first round of judging. During this round, the judges will be considering appearance. The top four cakes will be selected, after which everyone except the judges must leave the pavilion. Next, the judges will complete the tasting round. The final step will be to announce the winner."

While Nancy droned on about the rest of the festival events and activities, such as face painting for the kids, concerts, boat tours, and the sailing race, I played games on my phone. My ears perked up when she mentioned the pet-costume competition.

"There will be fifteen dogs…and, uh, one cat walking the runway this year." She stared at her printout. "That can't be right," she said. "Whoever heard of a cat wearing a costume?" Mrs. Moto sat up in my lap and meowed loudly. Nancy looked in our direction and shook her head. "I should have known," she muttered. She took a deep breath, then continued. "All dog owners, and cat owners, should report to the main stage this Sunday at eleven a.m. sharp. And for goodness' sake, make sure all your pets are on a leash. The last thing we need is animals running around creating chaos."

The pack of dogs sitting next to the stage took this as their cue to show Nancy exactly how chaotic things could get as they streaked past her in pursuit of a squirrel. Empty chairs went flying, the microphone was yanked off the podium when the German shepherd got caught up in the cord, and a banner was knocked to the ground by the Labrador retriever. The older woman threw her hands up in exasperation before wrapping things up.

After ensuring that Mrs. Moto's leash was firmly clipped onto her harness and making sure to hold her tightly in my arms, we wandered over to watch her canine competitors chasing each other around a tree. "They don't stand a chance against you," I whispered to the calico. She blinked slowly at me in agreement.

The terrier skidded to a stop in front of us, dropped a tennis ball in front of

Scooter, and wagged his tail. Scooter tossed the ball across the lawn. The terrier bounded after it, then promptly ran back, clutching it in his mouth while the two Yorkies trailed after him. Mrs. Moto gazed down at the three dogs assembled at our feet and purred loudly. She leaped out of my arms and greeted the Yorkies like long-lost friends while Scooter and the terrier continued to play fetch.

"Frick and Frack, get away from that disgusting creature right this minute," a woman yelled sharply.

"Oh no, it's that crazy neighbor lady," I said to Scooter.

I watched as her long red braids snapped in the wind as she marched toward us. She bent down and clipped leashes on the two Yorkies and pulled them away from Mrs. Moto. "Didn't you get my letter?" she hissed. "That cat is supposed to stay away from me and my dogs." I expected Mrs. Moto to hiss back, but instead she rubbed against the woman's legs. "Now see what she's done! There's cat hair all over my new skirt."

I looked at the long patchwork garment she was wearing. It appeared to have been assembled from fabric remnants picked up at a secondhand shop. Although I had to admit the embroidery and beadwork embellishing it were impressive in a weird sort of way.

"But aren't you used to having dog hair on your clothes?" Scooter asked in a far more pleasant tone than I think I could have managed.

"It's hardly the same thing," she huffed. "My dogs go to a professional groomer every week. They don't shed. I daresay your cat has never been professionally groomed." She brushed the bottom of her skirt. "You can tell by all the fur she leaves everywhere."

"She's a cat. She grooms herself," I

said.

"Just keep her away from me," she said angrily. She pointed at a middle-aged man with a shaved head and goatee standing next to the stage who was chatting to Ned and Nancy. "My lawyer can explain everything. Mike, get over here," she shouted. Then she stormed off with Frick and Frack in tow.

Mike held his hands up as he approached us. "Sorry, it's just business, guys. Nothing personal against you or Mrs. Moto."

"I thought you specialized in wills and estate planning," Scooter said.

"That's what I mostly do, but when you're a lawyer in a small town like this, you end up dabbling in this and that." He lowered his voice. "I shouldn't say this, but don't worry too much about the letter. You've moved out of the condos, so there shouldn't be an issue anymore. She's just blowing off a little steam. She was mad when the chief wouldn't do anything about her complaint."

"I'm surprised the chief took our side," I said.

Mike smiled. "Well, it was probably less about you and more about her from Chief Dalton's perspective. My advice is to let it go. She's kind of a crackpot. One of those artsy types. No one takes her too seriously." He glanced at his phone. "Is that the time already? I've got to get going, but I'll see you tomorrow at the cake competition."

"I'm surprised he called his client a crackpot," I said to Scooter after Mike left. "Wasn't that a bit unethical?"

Scooter shrugged. "Unethical is probably an overstatement, but I'd worry if he were my lawyer. What would he say about me to other people?"

"I guess it's a good thing you already have a lawyer."

Scooter's shoulders slumped. "Well, about that. It turns out I'm in need of a new one. I just got an email that Tom's laid up in the hospital." He saw the expression on my face. "No, don't worry. He'll be okay, but he will be out of commission for a while. The timing couldn't be worse with this contract dispute I've got going on."

I squeezed his hand. "You poor thing. How about some ice cream to cheer you up?"

"Nice try," he said with a smile. "Remember, if we want to 'Live Healthy, Live Long, and Live Strong,' we have to say no to ice cream."

Well, we might have to say no to ice cream, but I could certainly say yes to the M&M'S in my purse when Scooter wasn't looking. I think better when I'm eating chocolate, and I needed to put my thinking cap on and figure out how I could help my husband. I had a funny feeling in my stomach that things were far more serious than he was letting on.

CHAPTER 4
THE SCIENCE OF LEGWARMERS

The next morning, Scooter and I stopped by the sports pavilion to drop off my cake. My adorable nerd of a husband carried my masterpiece while I kept a tight hold of Mrs. Moto's leash to make sure she didn't go wandering off again.

Nancy was standing by the entryway holding a clipboard. "You're late," she said. "I was just about to lock up."

"You said that everyone had to drop their cakes off by nine. It's nine now.

How can I be late?"

"Everyone else has been here already. You're the last."

"Last doesn't mean late," I said. "In fact, last is a good thing. Haven't you ever heard the expression, 'Save the best for last'?"

"In my experience, dear, people who quote that expression have poor time-management skills. You might want to try setting your clock ahead by fifteen minutes. It's a trick I used with my kids when they were growing up. It ensured that they were never late."

"But I'm not late," I said. "I'm right on time."

Nancy looked at her watch. "It's three minutes after nine. You're late."

I narrowed my eyes. "I was here at nine on the dot. You're the one who made me late by spending three minutes talking about punctuality. Now, are you going to let me drop off my cake or what?"

She stared at me with those piercing blue eyes of hers for a moment, then wrote something down on her clipboard. "Fine, you can place your cake on the table with the others." As Scooter began to walk through the entrance, Nancy stopped him. "The only people who are allowed access to the pavilion are the bakers and me. The general public can join later when we commence the first round of judging."

"Oh, come on. It's not like this is Fort Knox. Let Scooter carry the cake in. It's a really awkward shape. I'm such a klutz, and I'm worried I'll end up dropping it."

Nancy shook her head. "Rules are rules. We certainly don't want a repeat of what happened last year, do we?"

"What happened last year?" Scooter asked.

"Some kids thought it would be funny to sneak in and steal one of the cakes. It was *not* funny. So this year, I'm closely monitoring who has access." She pointed at Scooter and Mrs. Moto. "The two of you stay out here." While Scooter and I awkwardly exchanged the cake for Mrs. Moto's leash, Nancy pursed her lips. "What exactly is that supposed to be?"

I looked at her incredulously. "You're kidding, right?"

"I don't kid, dear. I have no idea what that is."

"But it's from *Star Wars*."

"Never seen it." My jaw dropped. Someone who hadn't seen *Star Wars*. I didn't think that was possible. "Hopefully, it tastes better than it appears," Nancy said. "Gray frosting doesn't look very appetizing. Now, hurry up and put your cake on the table. It's already ten after nine."

* * *

"You seem like you're in shock," Scooter said as we walked toward the main stage. "Is it because Nancy has never seen *Star Wars*?"

"No, it's not that," I said. "Though that is hard to believe."

"Then what is it?"

I sighed. "It's Jeff's cake. I didn't think anyone would be able to top mine, but his is...I don't even know how to describe it. I've never seen anything like it before."

"Well, keep in mind that appearance is only fifty percent of the overall score. I'm sure you'll knock the judges' socks off in the tasting round."

"I wish you could have tried my cake. I had some cake scraps left after I cut out the pieces I needed. I turned them into cake pops with the leftover frosting."

"Personally, I'm glad you went to Alejandra's house to bake. As Trixie Tremblay says, 'It's easier to avoid temptation than to resist it.'" He stopped and looked at me. "You didn't eat one of those cake pops, did you?"

"No," I answered truthfully. I'd had three, not one. "It made things so much easier to cook in a real kitchen in a real house," I said. "It was sweet of her to offer after she heard about what I went through trying to bake on *Marjorie Jane*."

As we walked past the food booths, my tummy growled. I had abstained from breakfast that morning, telling Scooter that I was still full from the previous night's dinner. My stomach begged to differ. How was a bowlful of watercress, chia seeds, and Trixie Tremblay's special creamy rutabaga-tofu sauce supposed to have filled me up, especially when I could barely choke it down? Maybe that was the secret to the Rutamentals diet program. The food was so disgusting that you happily skipped meals.

"Stop staring at those hamburgers," Scooter said as he pulled me away from the Sailor's Corner Cafe booth. "I don't want to miss Ned's seminar."

"Oh, goody. A seminar on marine products. How fascinating."

Scooter nodded. "I know. It's going to be really interesting."

"You realize I was being sarcastic, right?"

Scooter looked crestfallen. "But I thought you were really getting into boating."

"There's a difference between sailing on a boat and fixing a boat. A *huge* difference."

"Hopefully, Ned's seminar will change your mind."

"I'm just hoping it takes my mind off Jeff's cake."

When we got to the main stage, there were hardly any chairs left. I was stunned. Maybe Scooter had been right, and marine products really were scintillating stuff. We snagged the last two open seats, sitting next to Wanda in the back row.

I glanced at her Trixie Tremblay–inspired outfit. "Aren't you hot in those legwarmers?" I asked. It was an unseasonably warm day for March, and I was already regretting wearing jeans.

"Well, a little," Wanda admitted. "But you can speed up your metabolism if you keep your ankles warm. It has something to do with the detoxification of your energy follicles. I don't really understand how it all works, but science was never my strong suit."

Wow, the science of legwarmers. And I thought I had heard everything. I was about to ask Wanda why she didn't also wear knitted wristbands, but a high-pitched squeal screeched through the loudspeakers.

"Sorry about that, folks," Ned said, looking flustered as he adjusted the microphone. He tucked his navy-blue Palm Tree Marina polo shirt into his pants, took a deep breath, and greeted the audience. "Welcome to the first in our series of safe-boating seminars. Today, we're going to talk about common marine products, the health and safety hazards they pose, and how to protect ourselves when working with them."

While Ned walked over to a table set up at the front of the stage, Wanda nudged me. "I'm really looking forward to this, aren't you?"

I did my best to appear noncommittal, which was easier than it sounded. While Wanda opened up a notebook on her lap, I noticed sweat dripping onto her flip-flops from the bottom of her legwarmers. It looked like some serious energy-follicle detoxification was going on.

"How many of you own this product?" Ned asked, holding up a large blue container.

Heads bobbed up and down. "We own that?" I asked Scooter.

"Of course," he said. "In fact, we own

ten of them. It was on sale at Melvin's last week."

I sighed. Ten containers of whatever that product was. Just what we needed. But it was my own fault. I had made the mistake of letting Scooter go to the local marine store by himself. Somehow, he always ended up maxing out our credit cards buying stuff for *Marjorie Jane* that we didn't need. Rather than worry about having willpower when it came to food, he would be better off learning how to just say no to the temptations at Melvin's.

While Scooter and Wanda focused on what Ned had to say about respirators, safety goggles, and work gloves, I managed to achieve a new high score on the latest game I had downloaded on my phone. I glanced over at Wanda's notebook. Not one single doodle, just pages and pages of extremely boring information written in very precise, compact letters. At least she had jazzed things up with a green gel pen and tiny circles for the dots over her *i*'s and *j*'s.

"Okay, I'll open it up to questions now," Ned said. "Raise your hand, and one of my helpers will make their way over to you with a microphone."

After a few questions on how to keep your pets from ingesting toxic chemicals (that was mine), the legal ramifications if you spilled diesel into a body of water (Mike chimed in on this one), and what to do if you inhaled epoxy fumes (Scooter seemed oddly interested in this topic, which was worrying), Jeff rose to his feet. "Excuse me, mate, but isn't the proper ratio three to one when using that, not two to one like you said?"

"You mean when you're using this?" Ned asked, holding up a bottle with a pump handle. Jeff nodded. "Yes, normally three to one would be correct, but in certain applications, you'll want to go with two to one instead."

"Yeah, I think you might have that

backward," Jeff said.

Ned frowned as he peered at the back of the bottle. "Uh...I don't think so. It says right here, two to one when you're..." His voice trailed off as he squinted at the label.

"You're probably reading that wrong," Jeff said as he bounded up the steps to the stage. When he reached Ned, he grabbed the bottle out of his hand and put his arm around his shoulders. "Totally understandable, mate. It's hard to see the fine print when you get to a certain age. No shame in reading glasses."

Jeff proceeded to tell the audience all about ratios for different products. Wanda's ankles continued to sweat profusely while I got a headache from all the math involved. Then he started describing tips and tricks he had learned from watching YouTube videos.

Scooter leaned over. "I've seen that YouTube channel. It's a couple of twenty-something kids who bought a sailboat without ever having been on one before and having virtually no sailing experience."

"Sounds familiar," I said dryly. "Except for the age part. Change that to a middle-aged couple and you'd be on to something."

Scooter stared at me blankly. "Huh?"

"That guy's a bit of a know-it-all," Wanda said as she adjusted her legwarmers. Scooter nodded in agreement.

"I hate know-it-alls," I said. "People always think they know better than the experts. Take Chief Dalton, for example. Just the other day, I was telling him the latest statistics on UFO sightings, and he completely dismissed me out of hand. He should just stick to handing out parking tickets and leave alien investigations to the pros."

Scooter laughed. "Not exactly the same thing, my little Milk Dud."

"I thought you were going to come up with a new pet name for me."

"I'm working on it. But I want to make sure I get it just right."

I was afraid Jeff was going to keep prattling on and on, but fortunately he broke into a coughing fit when he opened up one of the canisters to demonstrate something. I guess Ned was right—some of the fumes from marine products were bad for your health.

Ned took that as his opportunity to wrap things up. "We're out of time, folks. But if you have any more questions, please feel free to come up to the stage and chat. You can also have a look at the various products we talked about today."

Both Wanda and Scooter shifted in their seats, eager to run up front and check everything out in more detail. "And don't forget to enter the drawing for a hundred-dollar gift voucher to

Melvin's Marine Emporium," Ned added. "I'll be handing out the entry forms. Just put your name, phone number, and email address down, and we'll draw the lucky winner next weekend."

Scooter whistled appreciatively. "A hundred dollars. Imagine what we could buy with that." I shuddered as I pictured all the bottles of marine products we didn't need that he would want to add to our already extensive collection.

* * *

While Wanda and Scooter hustled up front to enter the drawing, I rummaged in my purse for some pain relievers. I washed a couple of tablets down with some water, then surreptitiously tore open a bag of M&M'S.

"Oh, if you like those, you're going to love the cupcakes I have for sale at our booth." I looked up and saw Penelope. She was wearing one of her trademark

Sugar Shack purple polka dot aprons over a white sundress. "They have miniature M&M'S inside, and they're frosted in bright colors like the candy. Want me to set one aside for you?"

Hmm. If you scrape the frosting off a cupcake, it's basically a muffin, and everyone knows muffins are healthy, right? Could I convince Scooter of that logic? Probably not.

"Sure. How about a blue one?" Penelope nodded. "But, if you don't mind, can we keep this between ourselves? Scooter and I are doing that Rutamentals diet."

"I don't think you're allowed to have cupcakes if you're on Rutamentals," Penelope said.

"Well, I'm pretty sure that's a technicality," I replied. "Just set one aside for me, and I'll grab it when Scooter isn't watching."

She chewed her lip. "If he asks me directly, I'll have to tell him the truth. I wouldn't feel right lying to him." She frowned. "And you shouldn't lie to him either."

"Don't worry. It won't come to that."

"Okay," she said. "I can't wait to see your cake."

"You won't even notice it next to Jeff's," I muttered.

She sat in the chair next to me and smiled brightly. "I'm sure that's not true. Besides, you shouldn't compare yourself to everyone else."

"But it's a competition. Comparison— that's the whole point. The judges compare the cakes and decide which one is the best."

"If I had my way, we wouldn't hand out prizes."

"Don't tell me. You're one of those participation-ribbon kind of people, right?"

"Sure. The important thing is trying, don't you think?"

"Trying to win," I said. "Maybe you

better save me two cupcakes. I have a feeling I'm going to need more than one after I lose out to Jeff."

Before she could try to convince me that winning wasn't everything, the chocolate Labrador bounded over to us and dropped a coconut at Penelope's feet. The Lab wagged her tail so enthusiastically that I was afraid she would knock a passerby over.

"Hello, Chloe," she said, scratching the dog's head. "Did you bring me another coconut?" She turned to me. "Chloe is crazy for coconuts. She loves husking them. Her owners give me the meat that's inside for my coconut pies."

Penelope bent down and inspected the coconut. "Seems like you need to do a little more work on this one." Chloe nudged her hand out of the way, grabbed it in her mouth, and sat under a nearby tree, holding the coconut between her paws.

"Looks like she's got company," I said,

smiling at the pack of dogs surrounding Chloe.

"That one's named Chica," Penelope said, pointing at the German shepherd. "And those two Yorkies are—"

"Frick and Frack," I said. "We're acquainted. Or should I say Mrs. Moto and the two of them are acquainted."

"Do you think your cat would get along with a dog?" Penelope asked. "See that terrier over there? Bob's not crazy about the water, and his humans are heading off to the Bahamas soon on their boat."

"We've barely got enough room on our boat for the three of us. I can't see getting a dog. But I know someone who might be interested. Do you know Jeff? He was talking about getting his fiancée a dog to keep her company when he travels." I spotted the young couple by the stage talking with Scooter. "That's them over there."

"I've seen him at the bakery before, but she doesn't seem familiar."

"She's not a local. She lives on Destiny Key. Ever been there?"

"When I was in elementary school, one of my friends invited me to spend the weekend at her family's cottage on the island, but my mother refused. She got really worked up about it. Funny how that memory has stuck with me. Maybe one of these days I'll get out there. But first, I better head back to our booth and tuck those cupcakes away for you."

* * *

The crowd had thinned out at the main stage. Only the true diehards seemed to be left discussing marine products. Ned, Wanda, Jeff, Mike, and Scooter were clustered around the table debating the merits of different brands of epoxy. Emily was leaning against the podium looking bored. I feared she was going to be marrying into a lifetime of sailboat obsession on Jeff's part. I'd have to invite her out for a girls' night and commiserate.

"Can you clear some room on that table?" Nancy asked as she climbed up the steps holding several large cardboard boxes. "These are heavy." She was followed by our restraining-order crazy neighbor lady, also bearing boxes.

After Ned moved the marine products to the side, the two of them set their boxes down. "Are those for Sofia?" he asked.

"Yes," Nancy said. She lifted the lid off the top box. "Can you believe how many bottles she has in here? This is just a small-town festival. There's no way she'll sell that many." Nancy held up a small brown glass vial and inspected the bottom. "She forgot to put the price stickers on them. That's what happens when you're not organized."

Ned reached into another box and

took out an envelope. "Are these the ones?"

Nancy pulled out a sheet of labels. "Yes, those are them. See how she used pink stickers in the shape of a sailboat? She printed these up especially for the festival." While Ned took the bottles out of the box, she affixed the stickers.

"What are these?" Emily asked.

"Herbal remedies," Nancy said. "Our daughter has a business selling them online. She also exhibits at fairs like this one, selling them in person."

"Is she the one who makes ointments and balms from plants in her garden?" I asked. "You gave me one of those to try once. It worked wonders."

"I've tried some of them too," Mike said. "Highly recommended."

Nancy beamed. "I'm glad you liked them. There's some of those in one of the other boxes. But the bottles, like this one, she imports from an overseas supplier. You all should stop by her booth later. She has something for everything that ails you." She held up a bottle. "This one is for chronic snoring. Just two drops in a cup of chamomile tea at night, and your partner will thank you for it. It's made a world of difference since Ned started taking it."

"There's no need to tell everyone about that," Ned muttered.

Scooter looked on in interest as Nancy described a concoction that suppressed your appetite. I wondered if it had rutabagas in it.

"Do you have anything for headaches? I took some pain relievers earlier, but they aren't doing the trick." I asked.

"I think there's something in here for that." She rummaged through a box, then pulled out a clear bottle with a stopper top. "Just a couple of drops on your tongue, and your migraine will be gone in no time."

"Oh, it's not a migraine, just a tension headache," I said.

"You need to be careful with these things," Jeff said. "They aren't regulated."

"Mr. Know-It-All," Wanda said under her breath.

"He's right," Emily said. "I would never touch any of those. Not in a million years."

"They're perfectly safe," our former neighbor said. "You just need to use common sense."

"It's a bunch of pseudoscience," Jeff said. "And some of this stuff is downright dangerous."

"You've been brainwashed by Big Pharma," she retorted. "I could give you all sorts of examples of doctors prescribing medicines their patients don't need just to satisfy the pharmaceutical industry. And half the time they don't even think about drug interactions."

Jeff said. "That's a bit harsh, don't you think? People in the medical field are trying to heal people, not harm them."

"Line their pockets is more like it!"

Emily laid her hand on Jeff's arm, but he yanked it away. "You sure could use some—"

Before he could finish his thought, the pack of dogs ran across the stage—correction, a pack of dogs and one very familiar-looking Japanese bobtail cat—and darted under the table, causing one of the legs to collapse. All the boxes fell onto the ground, spilling their contents everywhere. As we scrambled to pick everything up, I saw a flash out of the corner of my eye.

"Say cheese, everyone," Alan said, holding up his camera. At least I think that's what he said. It was hard to hear over the dogs barking.

"Alan, put down that camera and come over here and help," Nancy ordered. "The organizing committee hired you to take publicity shots of the festival, not pictures of scenes like this!"

CHAPTER 5
MATH-INDUCED HEADACHES

After everything had been cleaned up, those of us involved in the cake competition made our way over to the sports pavilion while Ned and the crazy neighbor lady carried the boxes of herbal remedies over to where the booths were set up.

The pavilion consisted of one large room, which was normally used for exercise classes. A poster on the double doors at the entryway advertised an early-morning Trixie Tremblay boot camp. At the rear of the building, near the door leading out to the enclosed courtyard, there was another poster— this one extolling the virtues of wearing legwarmers.

If I had fingernails to chew, I would have devoured them while I watched the judges file into the room with their clipboards in hand. I paced back and forth while I admonished the butterflies in my stomach. *Guys, you're getting out of hand*, I told them. *If you don't knock it off, I'm going to down one of Scooter's rutabaga smoothies. We'll see how you like that.*

Nancy had set up a barrier for members of the general public to stand behind while the judges appraised each cake and asked the contestants questions. My creation was the last on the table—because I had dropped it off right on time as I saw it or late as Nancy saw it—so I got to hear the judges' comments on the other entries before they reached mine.

They began with the twins' cakes. "I see you made German chocolate again this year, Gretchen. It's nice to see the official Coconut Cove cake represented today," Nancy said. She jotted something down, then peered over her reading glasses at Gretchen's sister. "And Gertrude, what do you have for us today? A classic white cake with buttercream frosting. Very nice."

Nancy was awfully generous in her praise of the ordinary, obviously made-from-a-box mix cakes. Had the twins bribed her? If so, what could one possibly bribe Nancy with? The crotchety old lady seemed to love only two things in the world besides her family—organizing people and things and rules and regulations. Wait a minute, was that two things or four things? My math-induced headache was getting worse.

While I rubbed my temples, Norm

came up behind the twins and put his arms around their shoulders. "How about a picture of me with these two lovely ladies?" he said to Alan. "Make sure you get my good side. Wait a minute, I don't have a bad side." He laughed, not seeming to notice no one else joined in. "Now, you two ladies are going to vote for me in the election, aren't you?"

"Really, Norm," Nancy said. "We're here to judge cakes, not campaign." She pointed at his clipboard. "Why don't you step aside, and let the chief and Penelope have a look at the entries while you fill out the scoring sheet."

Next up was Wanda. "Let's see, what do we have here? It certainly looks attractive," Nancy said. "Very skillful use of icing, dear. I could almost swear those vegetables on top were real. What are they made of? Marzipan?"

"No, they're real—baby peas, asparagus, and carrots. See how they spell out Rutamentals?"

Nancy adjusted her reading glasses. "Hmm...I've heard of carrots blended into cake batter, but never raw vegetables used as decoration, especially asparagus and peas."

Wanda held up a pamphlet. "This is Trixie Tremblay's newest creation, the RutaButaTooting Gâteau—designed for celebrations of all kinds. Anyone who's interested in 'Living Healthy, Living Long, Living Strong,' let me know, and I'll be happy to give you a brochure that includes the recipe for this cake plus a voucher for twenty percent off the Rutamentals program."

Nancy grabbed the brochure, walked over to the trash can, and threw it in. "Just in case I wasn't clear, this is a cake competition, not a campaign stop or an opportunity to sell the latest diet fad." She glared at two young boys who were tossing a ball back and forth in the back of the room. "Let alone a place to play games."

Scooter walked over to the barrier, leaned down, and removed the brochure from the container. While he eagerly read the recipe, I watched as the judges moved on to Mike's cake. He had gone with a classic chocolate fudge creation. While I'm sure it tasted delicious—it was made with chocolate, how could it not?—his decoration was pretty plain. Chocolate frosting with a few chocolate shavings on top wasn't exactly the stuff of gourmet magazines. Things were looking up. So far, three ordinary cakes and one cake made of vegetables.

Next up was the surly teenager. Her parents were in the audience cheering her on. Her father was holding up a banner while her mother was waving pompoms. The teen mumbled one-word answers to the judges' questions about her cake. "How much cola did you use?" Penelope asked.

"I dunno. Ask my mom. She made it."

The audience gasped. You would have thought it was the scandal of the year. Alan snapped pictures as the girl and her parents left the building in shame after she was disqualified.

Five down—one more to go before they got to my cake. I took a deep breath as the judges gathered around Jeff's masterpiece. He had created an entire ocean scene complete with a sailboat, dolphins, and a tropical island. Intricately decorated fish dotted the side of the cake, giving the illusion that they were swimming underneath the water.

"This is truly impressive," Nancy said. "How long did this take you to make?"

"Not long," Jeff said. "It's all a matter of skill and natural talent, and I have both of them."

"Where did you get the idea?" Penelope asked.

"I saw it on a YouTube video."

"The attention to detail is amazing,

son," Norm said. "We'll have to talk later about you catering my mayoral victory party."

The judges spent an extraordinary amount of time examining Jeff's cake and making notes. Finally, they turned to mine. Nobody said a word. It was an unnerving kind of silence. I couldn't tell if they were dumbstruck by the sheer creativity of my cake or if they hated it.

Finally, Penelope broke the silence. "What did you use to get the different shades of gray in your icing?"

"It's a special food dye," I said.

"It certainly is...um, gray," Nancy said as she scribbled notes. "But I still don't know what it's supposed to be. It just looks like a large gray ball."

Norm laughed. "You mean you don't recognize this? It's from *Star Wars*. Leave it to the kooky UFO alien lady to make a cake that resembles the Death Star."

"Nancy's never seen *Star Wars*," I

said.

"Really?" Norm and Penelope said in unison.

"Do you know what this is?" Nancy asked the chief.

He raised his dark, bushy eyebrows and after a long pause said, "Yes. My ex-wife is a big *Star Wars* fan. This is the kind of thing she'd like."

"Really?" I said. "I'd love to meet her one day."

Nancy gave me a funny look before collecting the clipboards from each of the judges. She added up the scores while the four of them conferred in a corner of the room. At one point, Nancy pointed at my cake and scowled. After fifteen of the longest minutes of my life, the judges reassembled in front of the audience.

"I will now read the names of the four individuals who are going to advance to the next round, in no particular order," Nancy said. "Please step forward when I call your name." Nobody was surprised when she read Jeff's name off. While the audience clapped, Emily leaned over the barrier and gave him a congratulatory kiss. Mike beamed when his name was announced next.

I took a deep breath. With the disqualification of the teenaged girl, it was down to the twins, Wanda, and me. While I tried to calculate my odds, making my math-induced headache even worse, Nancy called out Wanda's name. I was stunned. How could anyone vote for something that featured raw vegetables?

"And now for the final cake," Nancy said dramatically. The sisters held hands and looked nervously at each other. I reached into my pocket and pulled out my lucky key chain—the one with a tiny Wookiee attached. "The gray"—she paused while she peeked at her notes—"Death Star made by Mollie."

"That's my girl!" Scooter shouted while

I jumped up and down with excitement.

"If it were up to me, everyone would advance to the next round," Penelope said as she handed the twins back their cakes and ushered them to the other side of the barrier. "You ladies should be very proud of yourselves."

"Shush, everyone," Nancy said, clapping her hands. "It's time to cut the cakes. Norm, make yourself useful and bring that tray of plates over here."

While Norm tore himself away from schmoozing with the audience, Nancy explained the next stage in the competition. "Four slices will be cut from each cake and placed on different-colored plates, one color for each judge."

"Can I have the purple plates? It's my signature color," Penelope said as she smoothed down her apron.

"Of course, dear. Chief Dalton, you'll have the blue plates. Norm, you'll have the green ones, and I'll take the white ones."

Nancy sliced the cakes while Norm handed her a different-colored plate for each judge. After she set the slices on each plate, Penelope and the chief carried them over to four small tables at the back of the room, one for each judge. When she got to Jeff's cake, she startled when Bob the terrier ran into the pavilion. Her hand slipped, smudging the frosting and knocking one of the fish decorations off the final slice and onto the floor.

"Get that mutt out of here!" she yelled before placing the slice onto a purple plate.

Emily leaned over the barrier. "That slice looks terrible," she said to Nancy. "You should cut another one."

"It's fine, babe," Jeff said. "The judges already know how it's meant to look." He winked at her. "Knowing your sweet tooth, you probably want Nancy to cut another slice so you can eat the one that's missing a fish."

"That's right, dear. We've already completed the appearance round. Now we're onto the tasting round. It will taste exactly the same as another slice." She glanced at her watch. "Besides, we're running behind schedule. The judges will take a twenty-minute break, then reconvene here for the cake tasting. That portion of the competition will be closed to the public."

After ensuring the judges' tables were set up correctly, Nancy shooed everyone out of the pavilion. Emily continued to complain about how Nancy had ruined Jeff's cake. "I'm going to go back in there and cut another slice," she said. But when she tried to reenter the building, Nancy locked the door.

"As I said, young lady, only judges from this point forward."

Jeff put his arm around Emily's shoulders. "Don't worry about it. After all —"

"Fire!" someone yelled. "Fire over by the food booths!"

As gray smoke wafted overhead, cell phones started ringing, and people frantically looked for their loved ones.

"Everyone who's a volunteer firefighter, come with me," Chief Dalton shouted above the din. "The rest of you stay back and out of the way." Norm and the other volunteer firefighters ran after the chief, while everyone else followed more cautiously. Everyone, that was, except Jeff, Emily, Scooter, and me.

Emily rattled the doorknob angrily. "I can't believe she locked the door."

"It's almost like she doesn't trust us," I said dryly.

"Did you leave something in there?" Scooter asked.

"I didn't," the young woman replied. "Nancy did. She left a piece of cake that's all messed up. I need to go fix it."

"Babe, just let it go," Jeff said, pulling

her away from the door. "Why don't we go see what the fire's all about, like everyone else at the festival."

"But—"

"No buts," he said. "One little missing decoration isn't going to hurt my chances. You saw the competition. It's pretty amateurish. Of course I'll win first place." He glanced over at me sheepishly. "Sorry, Mollie."

Emily seemed embarrassed. "He didn't mean it like that. I really liked your *Star Wars* theme. Was it hard to get it into a spherical shape?"

"I used to have a special set of cake pans, but we lost them in the..." I paused to listen to the sound of fire engines pulling into the park.

"Lost them in what?" Emily asked.

"A fire," Scooter said softly. "We lost everything." He took a deep breath. "Why don't you two head over and see what's going on. I think we'll wait here. I don't have any desire to see another fire again any time soon."

Before they left, Emily tried the handle again. I thought about showing her alternative ways of opening doors that didn't involve keys but decided against it. Jeff would have probably jumped in and told me he was a black-belt-level cat burglar, having learned the trade through watching YouTube videos.

After they left, Scooter and I sat at a picnic table by the entrance. We both spent the next hour on our phones. I played my game, and he replied to several emails. While I was massaging my fingers—gaming was hard work—I saw a familiar ball of fur streak past the table toward the water.

"Didn't Ben take Mrs. Moto back to the marina after the boating seminar?" I asked.

"Uh-huh," Scooter said without looking up from his phone.

"Are we sure about that?"

"Uh-huh."

"How sure?"

Scooter put his phone down. "Oh no. I'm afraid to ask."

"I think I just saw her run past. Calico cat, green eyes, with a bobtail. There aren't too many of them around Coconut Cove."

Scooter shook his head. "Don't tell me she hitchhiked again." Mrs. Moto had many talents, one of which was sneaking into the backs of vehicles and going for rides around town. Somehow, she always managed to find her way back to the boat in time for dinner without fail.

"Wait here," I said. "I'll go investigate."

I walked behind the sports pavilion through a gate into the fenced-off courtyard and peeked into the restrooms located in an adjacent outbuilding. Nothing. I poked around in the shrubs, calling out her name and promising treats. No response. I turned to head back out front when I noticed the back door of the pavilion was slightly ajar. As I reached out to push the door open to investigate, Mrs. Moto tore past me toward the waterfront.

"Get back here this instant," I yelled. "There's extra catnip in it for you!"

She ignored my attempted bribe and made her way toward the fishing pier, no doubt to vacuum up scraps of fish and bait. As I started to climb the steps, she darted through the rails and scampered down the rocky embankment under the pier and onto the sand. "We're going to get you an industrial-strength leash and straitjacket for a harness if you keep this up," I yelled after her.

Before I could chase her down the beach, I tripped and landed on the jagged rocks, scraping both of my knees. It hurt like the dickens, but I quickly forgot my pain when I lifted my head.

There was Emily lying on the

embankment, convulsing violently. As I rushed over, her convulsions stopped, her head fell to the side, and her eyes turned glassy. I quickly dialed 911, then administered CPR to the unconscious woman until the EMTs arrived and took over.

I watched in horror as they tried to revive her before shaking their heads in regret. As they transferred her body to the ambulance, I wondered what could have caused someone to die at such a young age. I wasn't the only one who was curious. While most people were over gawking at the fire, a few of the guys who had been fishing on the pier were milling about, trying to get a glimpse of the scene and asking me what had happened.

I ignored their questions, slumped down on the beach, and put my head in my hands. Visions of what I had witnessed flashed through my mind— poor Emily lying on the rocks with a shattered plate by her side.

Wait a minute. A shattered plate, just like the ones that had been used for the judges' slices of cake. What had she been doing eating cake by the fishing pier?

CHAPTER 6
DOGS WITH KRAUT

"Scooter, are you okay?" I asked, noting his clammy skin and shaking hands.

"Is she..." His voice trailed off as he watched the ambulance pull out of the parking lot.

"I'm sure she'll be fine," I said, telling Scooter what he wanted to hear rather than the truth, for fear he'd go into shock. "They're taking her to the hospital now."

"But the lights and siren aren't on," he pointed out. "Please tell me you didn't find another—"

"You're trembling," I said, interrupting him before he had to say one of his least favorite phrases: "dead body." I knew he worried about my propensity for stumbling across people who weren't...let's see, how should I put this...people who weren't exactly alive. Since we had moved to Coconut Cove, I had found four dead bodies, all murder victims. Sadly, Emily took my total up to five. I didn't know the cause of death, but surely it couldn't be murder. Was I going to have to start keeping two separate scoring systems? One to tally up murder victims and one for people who died accidentally? I tried to figure out the statistical probabilities involved in finding so many dead bodies, but that made the throbbing in my head worse.

People were buzzing around, whispering about what had happened to Emily. Someone said that he'd go in search of Jeff. I didn't envy him that task. With the fire at one end of the festival and the commotion at the other end near the fishing pier, the police were spread thin. One of the officers had asked me a few questions before rushing off to coordinate with her colleagues.

Scooter looked miserable. I guided him toward a picnic table. "Here, sit down before you faint." I pulled a bag of M&M'S out of my purse and handed them to him. "These should help."

He ripped open the bag and began popping some of the colorful candy-coated chocolates in his mouth before he caught himself. "Do you have any healthy snacks instead?" he asked. I shook my head, wondering what had happened to my husband, who had always reached for chocolate when he was stressed. Nobody should stick to a diet in times like this.

"No, that's not something I normally carry." I dug through my purse. "How about a breath mint?"

Scooter raised his eyebrows. "Do you have any idea what's in those? Why not just inject poison straight into your bloodstream instead?" He held out his hand. "Give those to me."

"No way. There's a kosher hot dog piled high with sauerkraut, relish, mustard, and onions with my name on it at Alligator Chuck's food stand. I'll be needing a mint after scarfing one of those babies down."

Before I knew what was happening, Scooter grabbed the mints from my hand and lobbed them into a nearby garbage can. "My, aren't you the feisty one, showing off your college basketball skills," I said. "I guess you are feeling better."

He rubbed his hands on his shorts. "Not really. I can't believe you found Emily like that. Admit it. She didn't make it, did she?"

"No, she didn't," I said simply as I

squeezed his hand. I thought back to the sight of Emily lying on the ground beside the broken plate. "I wonder if she had a heart attack. She was awfully young, but some families have a higher risk of heart issues at an early age." I sighed. "Poor Jeff."

"I wonder how long they were engaged for," Scooter said, squeezing my hand back.

I laid my head against his shoulder. "Remember how you proposed to me?"

"Me? You're the one who proposed."

"That's not how I remember it," I said. "Besides, girls don't propose to guys. It's the other way around."

Scooter spluttered, "But you're the one who asked me."

Before we could settle that little disagreement, a voice boomed out from the loudspeakers. "Attention: Scooter and Mollie McGhie, come collect your feline from the information booth immediately." Even if I hadn't recognized Nancy's sharp tone, the disdain when she uttered "your feline" would have given it away. After a beat, she added, "Attention: any felines not collected in the next ten minutes will be turned over to animal control."

I stood and pulled Scooter to his feet. "Come on, we better go collect *our feline* before she disappears again." In the aftermath of finding Emily's body, I had lost sight of her. "After that, what do you say to those dogs? Surely, Trixie Tremblay would understand that in a situation like this, junk food is called for."

"There was a fire at the food stands, remember?"

"It's all okay now. I overheard the police officers saying it was an electrical fire at the Rutamentals stand. Wanda was using the patented Rutamentals high-speed, industrial-strength Rutablender to make fresh rutabaga shakes. Guess what she uses instead of ice cream—tofu. Yuck, right?"

"Is she okay?" Scooter asked.

"She's fine, and everyone is back in business."

"Good. That means we can get something that's Rutamentals-compliant at her stand." He tugged at my hand. "Come on, let's get going before Nancy has a fit."

We found Mrs. Moto sprawled out in front of the information booth surrounded by a bunch of kids who were taking turns scratching her belly. Nancy looked at her watch when she saw us approaching. "You're lucky you got here when you did. Another thirty seconds, and animal control would have taken her away."

A young girl scratched the calico behind her ears, then looked up at Nancy. "You wouldn't have really given Mrs. Moto away, would you have, Grandma?"

Nancy pursed her lips. "People need to be prepared to face the consequences for their actions, Katy. Animals need to be on-leash and supervised, as Scooter and Mollie well know." She looked at us sharply. "Rule 11.3 of the town charter. You do have a copy of the town charter, don't you?"

"No, but I'll be sure to get a copy and place it right next to my copy of the Palm Tree Marina rules and regulations," I said. Of course, what I didn't tell Nancy was that I had turned the marina rules and regulations into origami birds that Mrs. Moto liked to bat around when she wasn't busy chasing lizards.

Katy picked Mrs. Moto up and carried her over to her grandmother. "She says she's sorry, Grandma, and it won't happen again," she said before giving the cat a kiss on her head.

Nancy's expression softened. "All right, but you have to help keep an eye on her, okay?"

"Of course!" Katy said. "Maybe we can

bring her over to your apartment after school and keep an eye on her there."

I smiled at Nancy's discomfort. The last thing she wanted was to have *that feline* in her home.

"Thanks for taking care of her," Scooter said to Katy as he plucked our wayward cat from her arms. "We should probably go in search of something to eat. Something healthy, right, my little Milk Dud?"

Before I could try to persuade Scooter about the benefits of junk food, Ben rushed up. "There you are," he said, wagging a finger at Mrs. Moto. "I've been searching for you everywhere." He turned to us. "I'm sorry. I didn't realize she had sneaked into my truck until I got to the park and saw her darting out of the cab. Here's a spare leash and harness. I've been keeping it in my rig ever since she started hitchhiking everywhere with me."

After securing Mrs. Moto, Scooter set

her on the ground. She made a beeline for Alligator Chuck's food stand, which was conveniently located next to the information booth. Sitting in front of the stand was the usual gang of dogs, all waiting patiently in turn as the cook fed them each a piece of hot dog.

"Does it seem strange to be feeding hot dogs to dogs?" Ben asked. "Funny, there isn't any dish called hot cat."

"Don't let Nancy hear you. I'm sure she'd be tempted to come up with something."

We watched as Mrs. Moto pushed her way in front of the dogs, stood on her hind legs, and yowled. "Here you go," the young man said with a laugh as he handed her a morsel.

"Frick and Frack, come here," a gruff voice said. I turned and saw Chief Dalton glaring at them, both of his caterpillar-like eyebrows twitching furiously. "Here. Now."

The two Yorkies were torn—should

they stay with the nice dispenser of hot dogs or risk the wrath of the burly man? The chief took a step toward them and pointed at the ground in front of him. After the dogs slowly walked toward him, he bent down and scooped them up, one in each arm. Then, to my surprise, he kissed each of them on the head.

"What am I going to do with you? It doesn't do my reputation any favors if the two of you are running around off-leash." He set them on the ground and clipped them to matching leashes adorned with embroidery and beads. "Come on, let's get you fellows home. It's been a long day."

"Huh? You're taking them home? But they belong to our former neighbor," I said.

The chief arched one of his eyebrows. "We have joint custody."

"Joint custody? Wait a minute...does that mean that crazy lady is your ex-wife?" He arched his other eyebrow. "Wow. That explains so many things."

"What exactly does it explain?"

"A lot."

"Could you be more specific?"

"Tell you what, why don't you tell me what happened with Emily first. Was it a heart attack?"

"I don't believe you're the next of kin."

"Oh, that's a good point. Who is the next of kin?"

The chief snorted. "Don't turn this into one of your investigations."

"I'm not investigating anything. I'm just curious. Everyone is curious about what happened."

"Can I give them some more?" the cook interrupted, holding a couple of pieces of hot dog in his hand.

"No, they've had enough," the chief said. He looked down at the terrier, German shepherd, and chocolate Labrador. "Now, where are your owners?"

The three of them took that as their cue to run off across the park.

"Aren't you going to chase after them?" I asked. "They are breaking Rule 11.3 of the town charter, after all."

I glanced at Nancy. She seemed impressed. Sensing sarcasm was not her strong suit.

The chief suppressed a smile. "I'm surprised to hear you quoting rules and regulations, Mrs. McGhie, considering you usually think they don't apply to you." I was glad he got my sense of humor by now. He didn't always appreciate it, but he got it.

While the Yorkies and Mrs. Moto sniffed each other, tangling up their leashes in the process, the chief's phone rang. His expression sobered as he listened to the person on the other end of the line. "Copy that. Meet me at the information booth. Tell the medical examiner I'll call him shortly." After he hung up, he pointed at me. "You, with me. I've got some questions for you."

"About what?"

The chief raised one of his eyebrows, locked his eyes with mine, and didn't respond.

"Will they be multiple choice?" I prompted.

Then he raised his other eyebrow.

"True or false?" I tried to figure out what he was saying with his eyebrows, but even my phone didn't have a translation app for this. "It's not going to be an essay, is it?"

"The last thing I would ask you to do is write an essay. I can only imagine how creative your answers would be."

"Fine, just let me use the bathroom first." While I walked over to the restroom block, Scooter and the chief worked on untangling our pets.

After I washed my hands, I looked for some paper towels, but the ladies' room was out. I sneaked into the men's room and grabbed a few. As I was throwing them in the trash can, I noticed a small clear bottle with a stopper top. It looked exactly like one of the herbal remedies that Nancy had shown us earlier in the day.

When I rejoined Scooter, I showed him the bottle. "I found this in the men's room."

"What were you doing in the men's room?" he asked. "Was there a long line at the ladies'?"

"No, the place was deserted. I just needed some paper towels. For some reason, the men's always seems to have a good supply. Why don't guys wash their hands after they go to the bathroom?"

"That's not true. I do."

"Well, that's because your mother raised you right."

"What is that, anyway?" Scooter asked.

"It's one of those herbal remedies that Nancy was showing us earlier. This one is supposed to help with migraines." I peered at the back of the bottle. "It says you put two drops on your tongue." I shook the bottle. "It's empty."

"I guess the guy gets a lot of migraines, and he used the whole bottle up."

"But this is one of the ones that Nancy put labels on earlier. You can tell by the sailboat-shaped price sticker. That means someone used this whole bottle today. I wonder if there are side effects to such a big dose?"

Scooter shrugged. "I guess there can be side effects to anything."

"Remember how Jeff was talking about how this stuff isn't regulated? Do you think it's dangerous?"

"I'm sure it's fine. Come on, let's go. The chief has been waiting to talk to you."

"Where is he?"

"Getting a hot dog."

"Lucky guy. What about us? When are

we going to eat?" I asked in a slightly whiny tone. Hunger brings out my inner petulance.

"You know what, why don't we eat at home? I already have all the ingredients for a Rutamentals meal in the fridge. It'd be a shame to let it go to waste."

"Mrs. McGhie," the chief said, holding a dog with all the fixings in his hand. "Are you ready?"

"Remind me to ask Nancy about this later," I said to Scooter as I tucked the bottle in my purse. "Let's not make a decision about dinner yet, okay?" I turned to the chief. "I'm all yours."

* * *

"I'm starved," I said as we turned the corner onto Main Street. After answering questions from the chief about Emily's condition when I found her, then discovering that our car wouldn't start and waiting three hours for a tow truck that never showed up, we had decided to walk back to the marina. "I never did get my hot dog. I haven't eaten since breakfast."

"Intermittent fasting is good for you," Scooter said.

"Says who?"

"Scientists."

"You realize they make that stuff up just to get headlines."

"No they don't."

"Sure they do. When's the last time you read about how eating three chocolate bars a day is good for you?"

"Never."

"That's 'cause scientists are spreading fake news. You can't believe everything you read."

"Unless, of course, it says that an obscene amount of chocolate every day is good for you," he said dryly.

"Correct. Those are the kinds of headlines you can believe. Not that you ever see that because of the mainstream media's obsession with fruits and vegetables," I said. Scooter's stomach grumbled. "See, you're hungry too."

"That's not hunger. That's just my digestive system realigning itself."

"How about if we realign it with some Thai food? We can call in an order and pick it up on the way."

"Why would we do that? We've got Trixie Tremblay's rutabaga nut roast back on the boat, my little Milk Dud."

"Hmm...when you call me a little Milk Dud, do you know what that makes me think of? All my other favorite candies— M&M'S, Reese's Peanut Butter Cups, Hershey bars... Hey, is that your stomach growling again?"

"Not growling, realigning," Scooter said. His stomach continued to loudly "realign" itself. After a few moments, he dug his phone out of his pocket. "Fine, let's order Thai."

I grinned. Scooter's stomach and I

made a great team. "Pad thai for me, please," I said as he dialed.

"It's not going through. Let me see if I can get better reception across the street."

While Scooter went in search of more bars on his phone, I wandered over to Penelope's Sugar Shack to say hello to a few of my favorite friends in her display window—chocolate chip cookies the size of your head, éclairs crammed full of pastry cream, and apple fritters. It was a shame she was closed; I would have bought everything in sight.

As I eyed a particularly decadent-looking chocolate cream pie, I heard a gate creaking around the corner of the bakery.

Naturally, I decided to investigate. Maybe Penelope was walking toward the back entrance. Surely, she needed to offload those pastries since it was the end of the day, and I could get them at half price. Win-win for everyone. Plus, I never did manage to pick up those M&M cupcakes she had set aside for me.

Before I could walk through the gate, it swung shut. I was beginning to open it when I heard a woman talking. Someone who didn't sound like Penelope.

"You're late," the mystery woman said impatiently.

"What did you expect? I was at the hospital. Did you think I could just say, 'Sorry, mate, I know my fiancée just died, but I need to go meet someone at night in an alley.'"

That Australian accent was a dead giveaway—it belonged to Jeff. But who was he talking to? I pressed my ear against the wooden fence, earning myself a doozy of a splinter in the process.

"Stop pretending," the woman said. "It's not like you cared about her. You were just using her."

"Of course I cared about her. Would I

have proposed if I didn't?"

"She was loaded. That was the main attraction. Don't forget, I know all about your last fiancée and what happened to her."

"What happened? Nothing happened."

"That's not what I heard."

What happened to her? I wanted to ask. I felt like I was watching a soap opera in a language I didn't understand.

"It was an accident."

"You mean you convinced everyone it was an accident. It's not going to be so easy this time. They know she was poisoned."

"Why would I have poisoned Emily? Your logic doesn't make any sense. Since we weren't married yet, I wouldn't have inherited anything. It's certainly not in my best interests that she's dead." I stood on my tiptoes and tried unsuccessfully to peek over the fence. Sometimes, it sucked being short.

"Actually, if it's in anyone's interests

that she's dead, it's yours," he continued. "I'm sure the chief of police would be very interested to find out more about your connection to Emily and her family."

"You wouldn't dare," the woman said.

"Don't go stirring up any trouble for me, and I won't stir up any for you."

"Hey, where'd you go?" I heard Scooter call out.

"Somebody's here," the woman said. "I'm getting out of here. The last thing I want is to be seen with you."

I flattened myself against the wall and behind a hedge. Thankfully, I was wearing a dark top and jeans, which helped me blend in against the dark-purple siding. The gate creaked open. With the hedge in my way, all I could see were the legs of the person who was leaving. I'd recognize those flip-flops and legwarmers anywhere—it was Wanda, without a doubt. Questions flooded through my head. What was

Wanda's relationship to Emily? What had happened to Jeff's first fiancée? And more importantly, who had murdered Emily?

CHAPTER 7
EXTRA-CRISPY HASH BROWNS

After a sleepless night—nightmares about Emily being poisoned and monsters wearing brightly colored legwarmers kept waking me up—I was more than ready for an extra-large cup of coffee.

It was easier to convince Scooter to go for breakfast at the Sailor's Corner Cafe than I thought it would be. Maybe that was because he had fallen off the Rutamentals bandwagon the previous night with Thai food. Or maybe it was because my tossing and turning had kept him from getting a good night's sleep, and he knew that a Rise and Shine Smoothie just wasn't going to do the trick.

Even though it was early Sunday morning, there was a long line snaking out the entrance of the cafe. "Looks like it's going to be a bit of a wait," Scooter said. "Maybe we should go back to the boat and have smoothies instead."

The smell of bacon, hash browns, and coffee wafted out the door, causing my mouth to water. I had to act quickly before his willpower resurfaced. "Let me just have a peek inside. Maybe we can share a table with someone."

As I sidled past some tourists waiting to pay their checks, I accidentally knocked a carved wooden lighthouse off the counter. In addition to serving up tasty food, the Sailor's Corner Cafe also sold nautically themed artwork made by local artists. The walls were covered with paintings of fishermen, sailboats, and whales. The display cabinet by the cash register contained jewelry featuring starfish, dolphins, and sea turtles. I made a note to check out a particularly cute pair of sand-dollar earrings later.

As I was placing the carved lighthouse back on the counter, I spotted Penny sitting in a booth by the window leafing through a sailing magazine. "Are you by yourself?" I asked.

"Yes," she said. "Ben was supposed to meet me, but he just texted to say he's not going to make it. I assume Scooter is around here someplace. Why don't the two of you join me?"

"I was hoping you'd say that." I slid onto the opposite bench and tapped on the window to get Scooter's attention. I pointed at Penny and gave him a thumbs-up. "Have you ordered yet?" I asked as I picked up a menu.

"No. It's crazy in here today, and they seem to be short-staffed." She glanced around the room. "I don't recognize anyone. Guess it's mostly out-of-towners here for the festival."

"I think you spoke too soon," I said. "Looks like Norm over there."

"Whatever you do, don't make eye contact," Penny said. "If I have to listen to him stumping one more time, I'm going to lose it."

"Anyone would be better than him as mayor. Even a dog."

Penny laughed. "Now there's an idea. What if we got a dog to run against him?"

"What are you two ladies giggling about?" Scooter asked as he slid into the booth next to me. After we explained our plan to elect Coconut Cove's first canine mayor and brainstormed ideas for campaign slogans ("Bark for a Better Tomorrow" and "Chihuahuas for Change" were some of my favorites), one of the harried waitresses, Alejandra Lopez, came to take our order.

She wiped down our table, then gave us a tired smile. "Sorry it took me so long to get to you. But don't worry, when I saw you come in, I put orders in for your usual—oatmeal for Penny, Denver omelet, sausage, and extra-crispy hash browns for Scooter, and of course pancakes and bacon for Mollie."

Scooter's eyes grew wide. "Um… actually, I was wondering if I could change—"

I jabbed my elbow into his side. "What I think he means to say is thanks for looking out for us. If you hadn't, it would probably be at least an hour before we got served."

"No problem, *chica*. The three of you are some of my favorite customers," she said.

"Order up," the cook shouted as he placed two plates of waffles on the counter.

"I need to get that," Alejandra said. "I'll be back with some coffee in a jiff, and your meals shouldn't be too far behind."

Scooter leaned back in the booth and put his hand on his stomach. "I think I've gained five pounds just sitting in this place. I was going to be good and order the fruit salad and nothing else."

Penny laughed. "That sounds like something my mother would say."

"Hey, how is your mom?" I asked. "Is she still coming to visit this week to watch the sailboat race?"

"No, she can't come now," Penny said glumly. "I really wanted her to see *Pretty in Pink* in action."

"It would have been great for her to see us cross the finish line when we won," I said.

"Oh, please," Scooter said. "There's no way you ladies are going to beat us. *Naut Guilty* is going home with the trophy."

"I didn't realize you were crewing on Mike's boat," Penny said.

"Yeah, he texted last night to say he

needed another guy, so I volunteered."

Penny tapped her fingers on her lips. "Let's see if I have this right. This is the first sailboat that Mike's ever had. He used to be a powerboat guy. This is the first race he's ever entered. His crew is made up of people who don't have much sailing experience—"

Scooter interjected, "But I've sailed before."

"That was a million years ago," I said. "The only experience you've had lately is when we moved *Marjorie Jane* from her slip at the marina to the boatyard. Whereas I've been taking sailing lessons with Penny for a while now. And the other ladies on the crew have been sailing for years. There's no way *Naut Guilty* is going to win."

Penny and I high-fived each other across the table while Alejandra set three steaming mugs of coffee down. "Are you guys talking about the race too?" she asked. "It seems like that's on everyone's mind this morning. Norm is over there taking bets that his boat is going to come in first place."

"No, no, no," Scooter said as he placed his hand on my arm. "I can see what you're thinking. You want to make another bet with Norm."

"I sure do," I said. "I won the last one he made with me. I'd love to see the look on his face when I win this one too. Besides, with Penny as our captain, there's no way I can lose."

Alejandra bustled back with our meals. "Thanks again for letting me use your family's kitchen the other day to bake my cake," I said as I moved my coffee cup out of the way to make room for my pancakes. "It was so nice to have enough space to work in."

"No problem," she said. "Having a big kitchen is one of the benefits of still living at home with my parents. Saving on rent is another plus—gets me that much closer to saving up enough money to open up my own nail salon."

Penny gave Alejandra an encouraging smile. "Don't worry. It'll happen sooner than you think. And Mollie and I will be first in line for a manicure."

I held up my hands, showing off my short, unvarnished fingernails. "Good luck transforming these. Boat work has taken its toll."

"Challenge accepted," Alejandra said over her shoulder as she hurried back to the kitchen.

Scooter frowned while he stared at the mound of potatoes piled on his plate. As I reached for the maple syrup, I said, "Anyway, back to Norm. Care to place a side bet? If *Pretty in Pink* wins, you'll go back to eating normal food."

His eyes lit up. "And if *Naut Guilty* wins, you'll stop cheating. Don't think I don't know about the chocolate you've been carrying around in your purse."

"Deal," I said, shaking his hand. "Now, let's eat."

While Penny gobbled down her oatmeal and I polished off my pancakes and bacon, Scooter picked at his eggs, pushed his hash browns around his plate, and tried his best not to make eye contact with his sausage links.

Penny's phone buzzed. "I barely heard that over your tummy grumbling," she told Scooter.

"That's just his stomach realigning itself," I said. She gave me a quizzical look before checking her messages. I stuck a fork in Scooter's potatoes. "If you're not going to eat these, then I am. Extra crispy, just the way I like them."

Scooter pulled his plate away. "How can you still be hungry?" he asked. I smiled as he scarfed down the hash browns. "I'm just saving you from yourself," he said in between hurried bites.

Penny put her phone down. "That was Jeff. He wants to see some more boats."

"Really?" Scooter crumpled up his napkin and put it on his now-empty plate. "I would have thought he would be too broken up over Emily's death."

"Me too," Penny said. "But he seems more determined than ever. He's even decided to name his new boat *Emily Belle*, after her."

"That's sweet," I said. "Makes me wonder if our boat was named after a real Marjorie Jane."

"Sounds like another investigation for you," Penny said.

"Please don't encourage her." Scooter waved at Alejandra and pointed at his coffee cup.

"Speaking of investigations and Jeff, what do you know about him?" I asked.

Penny smiled. "How did we get from investigating the name of your boat to Jeff?"

While Alejandra refilled our cups, I tried to figure out what to say. On one hand, I didn't want Scooter to know I had accidentally overheard Wanda and Jeff talking about Emily the previous night. Knowing him, he might jump to conclusions and claim I was eavesdropping. But on the other hand, they had talked about how Emily had been poisoned, and each of them seemed to want to pin it on the other.

I needed to know more about Jeff's backstory and his relationship with Wanda. Of course, Scooter would say that I didn't really "need to know" anything about it, that it didn't involve me. But after eavesdropping on their conversation—oops, scratch that—after *accidentally overhearing* their conversation, I was obliged to follow up. You know what they say: "Do unto others as you'd have them do unto you." It's like paying it forward. If something mysterious ever happened to me, I'd want folks to investigate.

"Is it just me, or does Jeff have mismatched ears?" I asked. Okay, I know that seems like a random thing to say, but trust me, I had a plan with my line of questioning.

"You're investigating Jeff's ears?" Penny asked while Scooter rolled his eyes.

"I was just wondering if it's an Australian thing," I said casually. "That's where he's from, right?"

"Yeah, he moved here last year for work," Penny said.

"I heard a rumor that he had been engaged before Emily. Was it when he was back living down under? Has he said anything to you about that? Do you know why it ended?"

"You heard a rumor," Scooter said dryly. "Are you thinking his engagement broke off because of his ears?"

Penny scratched her head. "I've never noticed anything funny about his ears."

"What about his former fiancée?" I asked.

"No, I don't know anything about that,"

she said. "Our conversations have pretty much just been about boats."

"What kind of work does he do?"

"He's some sort of sales rep. Travels quite a bit for client meetings."

"With all that travel, he might not have had a chance to get to know that many people in Coconut Cove," I said. "Like Ned, Nancy, Ben or...uh, say, Wanda. Do you know if he knows them?"

"Not sure if he knows Ben. I introduced him to Ned and Nancy when he first came to the marina to check out boats."

"And what about Wanda?"

"Wanda met Jeff and Emily for the first time at the festival. I introduced them all at Ned's seminar yesterday."

"So none of them seemed to know each other beforehand?"

"No," Penny said. "Why are you so interested in who he knows?"

"Oh, well, I know how it is when you're new to town. It can be hard to meet people. I thought I could organize some sort of get-together for Jeff so he can get to know folks. It might also help him take his mind off Emily's death."

"That's so sweet of you," Penny said. "I'm sure he'd love that."

While she excused herself to go to the restroom, Scooter turned to look at me. "What exactly are you up to?"

"Me? Nothing," I said innocently.

"I'm guessing it's opposite day," he said. "Because when you say 'nothing,' I'm pretty sure you mean 'something.'"

"Aren't you late for your conference call?"

"Shoot, I am," he said. He stood and picked up the check from the table. "I'll pay this and meet you back at the boat later, okay?" After bending down to give me a kiss, he added, "And try to stay out of trouble."

"Sure thing," I said. Which was true. My next stop was to pay a visit to Chief Dalton and get him up to speed on my investigation. I couldn't exactly get into trouble doing that—could I?

* * *

Rumor had it the chief was at the beach by the Palm Tree Marina watching the kids' sailing races. Rumor also had it that the reason the chief and his ex-wife split up was because of a disagreement about what to name their dogs. Now I had two things to investigate—Emily's mysterious death and whose idea it was to name the Yorkies Frick and Frack.

I heard these rumors at Penelope's Sugar Shack. After the Sailor's Corner Cafe, it was the next best place to catch up on all the gossip and find out what people were up to. The young woman who made my mocha had told me where I could find the chief and the scoop on his marital woes.

Coffee in hand, I walked down the wooden steps leading from the Palm

Tree Marina to the sandy beach, which stretched from one end of the cove to the other. "Mind if I join you?" I asked.

The chief was sitting on a piece of driftwood. When he looked up at me, his bushy eyebrows twitched. "I don't suppose you'd ever take no for an answer."

"I think you're going to want to hear what I have to say." I plopped down next to him, taking in his outfit—navy shorts, a crisp short-sleeved shirt, and sandals. "I don't think I've ever seen you out of uniform. I'm surprised you're off duty at a time like this."

He shook his head. "I'm not off duty. The dogs were running circles around me, begging for a treat. I tripped over them and spilled iced tea all over myself. All my other uniforms are in the wash, so I've had to settle for civilian wear." He pursed his lips. "What did you mean by 'at a time like this'?"

"Aren't you investigating Emily's

death?"

"Why would I be doing that?"

"She was poisoned."

"Was she?"

"Yes. Everyone knows that."

"They do?"

"Wait a minute. I'm the one who should be asking the questions," I said, pulling a notebook and pen out of my bag.

The chief raised one of his eyebrows. "You should be?"

"See, there you go again." He raised his other eyebrow as he looked at my notebook. "What? You've never seen C-3PO and R2-D2 stickers before?" I asked.

He pointed at the kids who had finished their sailing race and were pulling their Optimist dinghies up on the shore. "I have, but usually with that age bracket, not yours."

"How do you know how old I am?"

He shrugged. "It's on your record."

"What record?"

"Are you denying that you have a record?"

I kicked off my flip-flops and scrunched my toes in the sand. "It was just a misunderstanding."

"A misunderstanding involving bolt cutters?" he asked.

"We have more important things to discuss than bolt cutters." I flipped open my notebook. "First, let's talk about what Emily was poisoned with. I assume you have the toxicology report back."

"No comment."

I scribbled a few notes down. "Okay, item number two—how she was poisoned. Was it an injection? Was it in something she ate or drank?"

"No comment."

"Fine. We'll move on to item number three. Who would have wanted Emily dead?"

"No comment."

"Did anyone ever tell you that you're

not a great conversationalist?"

The burly man frowned. "Yeah. My ex-wife."

"Tell you what—why don't we make this more of an interactive discussion. I'll tell you what intel I've come up with so far, and then you shed a little more light on the investigation."

"Fire away," he said.

"Okay. Jeff and Wanda are the prime suspects so far." That generated a few eyebrow contortions on the chief's part. I pulled a pencil out of my bag and made a quick sketch in my notebook.

"Is that a picture of me?" He pulled the notebook out of my hand and peered at it.

"Uh, maybe. You do know that you have very expressive eyebrows, don't you? It's almost like you communicate with them. Far more effectively than you do with words, I might add."

"Have you been talking to my ex?"

"She's the last person I'd want to

speak with after she threatened to file a restraining order against Mrs. Moto."

The corners of his mouth twitched. "Did she really go through with sending a letter?" Then he frowned and tapped the notebook. "Explain this picture, if you please, Mrs. McGhie."

"Just trying to decode the language of your eyebrows. I figure when you move them in certain ways, it must mean different things. Kind of like decoding raccoon sign language."

"I didn't know raccoons had eyebrows."

"They don't. It just reminds me of that time I was studying raccoon—"

The chief held up his hand. "Enough about eyebrows and raccoons. Honestly, I'm surprised you and my ex don't get along. You both have some really kooky ideas. Now, why don't you get back to what you were saying about Jeff and Wanda having a motive to murder Emily."

"Hah! You admit it. It was murder!"

The chief shrugged. "It'll be in the newspaper soon enough. That photojournalist, Alan, managed to get a video recording of one of the clerks at the medical examiner's office talking about it to a friend at the Tipsy Pirate. He keeps pestering me for more details. Remind you of anyone?"

"Nah. I've got a lot more personality than he does."

The chief bit back a smile before folding his arms across his chest. "Jeff and Wanda," he prompted. After I told him about the two of them knowing each other, despite pretending they didn't, Jeff's former fiancée, Wanda accusing Jeff of being a gold digger, and Wanda's mysterious connection to Emily and her family, the chief finally relented and shared a detail about Emily's murder.

"She ate a piece of poisoned cake. It was gelsemium that killed her," he said. "Also known as woodbine. Some people use it to treat certain conditions, but it can be very dangerous, even in small doses."

"So dangerous, it can kill someone," I said soberly, thinking about the convulsions Emily had been having when I found her.

The chief nodded. "That makes us square." He got to his feet. "Now, I better get back and feed and walk Frick and Frack before they tear the place up."

While he walked back down the beach toward the marina, I quickly scrawled down things to follow up on: (1) how did the killer get a hold of the gelsemium; (2) how did they know Emily would eat the cake; and (3) why did gelsemium sound so familiar?

* * *

"Where's Mrs. Moto?" Katy asked as she ran up the beach toward me. She was followed by her younger brother, Sam, who was using his towel as a superhero cape.

"She's back on the boat resting," I said. "She had a long day yesterday."

"Oh. I wanted to see her and tell her my good news," Katy said.

"What's that?"

"I came in first place in the under-ten division!"

"That's great," I said. "I saw the end of your race while I was sitting here. I'm going to be in my first sailing race on Tuesday. Do you have any tips for me?"

She thought about it for a moment, then said with a serious look, "Don't fall off the boat."

"Yeah," Sam echoed. "Don't fall!"

"Sound advice," I said. "I will try to stay on the boat."

"My uncle fell off a sailboat last year," Katy said.

"Oh no, that's terrible! Was he okay?"

The young girl tugged at the towel

wrapped around her waist. "Yes, but my aunt was really upset."

"I'll bet she was."

"She told him he wasn't allowed to go racing anymore. He didn't like that."

"I can understand that," I said, closing my notebook. "Is he your father's brother or your mother's?"

The two kids thought about that for a while. "Our dad's," they said in unison.

"He has lots of brothers and sisters," Katy added.

"What's a lot?"

Katy counted on her fingers. "One, two, three, four, five!"

"I wish I had brothers and sisters," I said.

She cocked her head to one side. "You don't have any?"

"No, I'm an only child."

"I wish I had another sister, instead of a stupid brother. It would be just like in the movie *Parent Trap*."

"Oh, I'm sure you don't mean that," I

said.

"I do!" Katy glared at Sam. "He put my Elsa doll in the washing machine and ruined her."

Sam looked down at the ground. "I said I was sorry," he said softly.

"Why don't you sit down and tell me about *Parent Trap*," I said, patting the driftwood on either side of me.

"We saw it with Grandpa," Sam said as he nestled against me.

"There were two twins—one lived with her mother and one lived with her father —and they didn't know about each other," Katy said. "They met at summer camp and discovered they were secret sisters!"

"Then what happened?" I asked.

"They trapped their parents into getting back together," she explained.

"We ate popcorn," Sam added.

"And cookies," Katy said. "But Grandpa said we weren't supposed to tell Grandma about the cookies.

Promise you won't tell her about the cookies either."

"I promise," I said solemnly. "I'm very good at keeping secrets. Speak of the devil." Nancy was standing on the boardwalk motioning at the kids. "You better scoot along."

I reflected on the upside of being an only child while they raced each other down the beach. My mom and I had fun watching *Parent Trap* together—the original, not the remake. I decided to send her a jokey text.

Remember Parent Trap? What's my secret twin sister's name?

I watched the gulls darting in and out of the surf while I waited for her response.

She sent a one-word text back, which probably took her five minutes to type.

Mary

Not the answer I'd expected. *Who's Mary?* I replied, then waited another five minutes.

Your twin sister

I looked down at my phone in shock. Was it possible I really did have a secret sister? The only response I could manage consisted of question marks. A few minutes later, my mom replied with her own series of question marks.

I tapped on my phone furiously. *How come you never told me I had a sister before?*

Don't be silly. You're the one who told me about her. Gotta go. Late for bridge.

After not getting a response to any of my subsequent texts, which mostly consisted of more question marks interspersed with exclamation points, I put my phone and notebook into my bag and felt something hard at the bottom. I pulled out the small, empty, stopper-topped bottle that I had found in the trash in the men's room the day Emily was killed. I peered at the label on the front. That's why it had seemed so familiar. It was the herbal remedy for migraines, also known as gelsemium, that Nancy had shown me the other day.

CHAPTER 8
RUTABUBBLES

I could barely drag myself out of bed the next morning. Nightmares had continued to plague me. This time they featured C-3PO and R2-D2 chasing after me with bolt cutters while I was running through the Death Star wearing a giant raccoon costume and holding a bottle of gelsemium.

I attributed my bad dreams to the herbal remedy I had found in my bag the previous afternoon. It completely freaked me out to know I had been carrying the possible murder weapon around with me, right next to my bag of M&M'S. The possibility of having a secret twin sister might have also been a factor in sleeping poorly. My mom still hadn't responded to my texts. She'd probably misplaced her phone yet again.

When I had dropped the bottle off at the police station yesterday, Chief Dalton had subjected me to a barrage of questions about when I had found it, what else I knew about herbal remedies, and what I was doing in the men's room. He wasn't amused when I kept replying, "No comment." In the end, I explained everything to him, including the fact that men's rooms never seem to run out of paper towels and that maybe his officers should investigate why some men think washing their hands is optional. He assured me that he practiced good hygiene.

I finally dragged myself out of bed, but

only because Scooter was talking about going to Melvin's to pick up a shore power cord adapter. Not only was I reluctant to let Scooter go to the marine store unsupervised but I also wanted to pick up some supplies. Somehow I had volunteered to be in charge of installing a new fuel filter and water separator system for our diesel engine. I blamed sleep deprivation for having agreed to take this project on. It was the only logical explanation. Well, there was also the fact that I had been hiding chocolate in the engine compartment that I didn't want him to find.

As we pulled up in front of the store in our newly repaired car, I noticed a sign in the window advertising for a store manager. Melvin had been through a lot in the past couple of months, and I was glad to see he was finally going to get some help. The high school kids who worked on weekends and after school were great, but it wasn't the same thing as having someone manage the store day in and day out. Maybe Melvin would finally have a chance to relax and be able to go back to the Bahamas to visit his family.

Scooter got sidetracked with a display of boating shoes, so I headed to the back of the store. While I tried to remember what model number I was searching for, I overheard two women talking about Emily's death.

Yes, *overheard*, not eavesdropped. I was in the engine systems aisle before they were. It's not like I was hiding somewhere listening in on their conversation. It's just that my ears perked up when one of them mentioned herbal remedies.

"See, what did I tell you? You shouldn't use anything unless your doctor prescribes it," the older woman said.

"Mom, lighten up. I only rub lavender oil on my temples at night. It helps me sleep better. It's not like I'm ingesting anything." She squeezed her mother's hand. "And I made sure to do my research before I started using it."

"That's the problem. People don't research these things. They just pick up a bottle. It says it'll cure your migraine or whatever else ails you, and they take it without a second thought. Would you have known what gelsemium was before that article in the newspaper? Would you have known what the side effects are and how dangerous it is if you have certain medical conditions?"

The younger woman pursed her lips. "I'm not sure. It did sound kind of familiar. Maybe it was on some sort of TV show?"

"You shouldn't get medical advice from TV." Her mother frowned. "TV or not, I don't think most people would have ever heard about it before. I'm telling you, whoever killed that poor girl knew exactly what they were doing."

When the conversation turned to less interesting matters—like why the young woman didn't come home to visit more often—I grabbed the equipment I needed and headed in search of my husband.

While I watched Scooter try on shoes, I considered what the mother had said. I certainly hadn't known what gelsemium was before yesterday. The killer must have gotten the bottle the day of the murder. Did they buy it from Nancy and Ned's daughter's stand? No, that didn't seem likely. Ned had mentioned that Sofia wasn't going to be setting up her stand until later that afternoon. Then I remembered what had happened after Ned's seminar. When the pack of dogs raced across the stage, the boxes with the herbal remedies had spilled on the ground. Could someone have pocketed one of the bottles?

I sat down on the bench next to Scooter and pulled my notebook out of my bag. Time to make a list. I chewed on my pen as I tried to remember who had been there. I wrote down their names—Ned, Nancy, Wanda, Jeff, Mike, Alan, the chief's ex-wife, and, of course, poor Emily.

Ned and our crazy former neighbor hadn't been at the cake competition, so I crossed them off the list. Besides, Ned didn't have a mean bone in his body, and someone who had been married to a police officer wouldn't be a likely suspect.

Nancy's name was the next to be scratched off. The last thing she would have wanted was for the cake competition to be ruined, not after she had spent so much time organizing it. Besides, what motive would she have had?

That left me with Wanda, Jeff, Alan, and Mike. I put stars next to the first two names. Wanda and Jeff definitely were hiding something, and both had a connection to Emily. Maybe Alan had also had a connection to Emily. She certainly seemed to have been avoiding him at the boatyard when Penny was showing boats to her and Jeff. I put a question mark next to the photographer's name. When I got to the next person on the list, Mike, I chewed my bottom lip. What possible link could there be between a small-town lawyer and a young woman from the remote island of Destiny Key?

* * *

"What are all these kids doing out of school on a Monday?" Scooter asked as he drove down Main Street.

"It's spring break," I said. "That's why they hold the festival during this part of March, so that families can attend events during the week. Lots of parents take the week off work."

"Smart thinking," he said. "Tourist

dollars are important to Coconut Cove's economy."

I adjusted my cardigan. "I'm glad it's not as hot as it was this weekend. Folks won't be rushing back to their hotels to soak up air conditioning instead of spending time at the festival. Hey, do you mind stopping here?" I asked, pointing at one of the gift shops lining the street. "We need to pick up your sister a birthday present, and I think she'd like one of those flamingo aprons they have for sale there."

"I completely forgot about her birthday," Scooter said.

"That's why you have me. Quick, a spot just opened up over there."

After parking the car, we crossed the street, dodging tourists carrying ice cream cones, hot dogs, and funnel cakes. "Hey, isn't that Mike coming out of the gift shop?" I said.

"It is. Perfect timing. I want to talk to him about referrals for contract lawyers."

It certainly was perfect. A perfect opportunity to speak with him about Emily's death.

After Mike gave Scooter a few suggestions of people to contact, he offered to have a look at the contract in question. "It's not my area of specialization, but maybe I can give it a once-over while you try to line someone else up to look at it more in depth. It can take a while to get a hold of these guys."

"That would be great," Scooter said. "I'm under the gun with this thing, and there are a few areas that are really concerning me. You could at least steer me in the right direction."

"No problem."

"You deal with wills and estates, right?" I asked. Mike nodded. "So what happens when a young woman like Emily dies without a will?"

"Well, it depends what state they're a resident of." He gave me a quizzical look. "But why do you assume she didn't have a will?"

"Oh, it's just that when I was her age, I didn't have one. I didn't even think about it."

"But you have them now, don't you?"

"We updated them recently to make a provision for Mrs. Moto," Scooter said.

Mike smiled. "You'd be surprised how many people mention their pets in their wills."

"So, in Emily's case, assuming she didn't have a will, who would her estate go to?"

"Well, her estate would get divided by a set formula determined by the state."

"Okay, so we know she wasn't married, both her parents are dead, and she was an only child. How would it work in that scenario?"

Perspiration began dripping down Mike's face, along his goatee, and onto his shirt collar. Wanda probably would have said his energy follicles were detoxifying. Maybe he needed some sort of neck warmer to soak up the sweat. "She was an only child?" he asked.

"Uh-huh. I thought you knew her?"

Mike shook his head. "No, not really."

"Hmm. Well, I think she was loaded. She mentioned having an estate. So there certainly have to be people interested in what happens to her money, right?"

Mike loosened his tie and unbuttoned his collar. "Listen, even if I knew, I couldn't say anything. You know, attorney-client privilege."

"I'm just asking hypothetically," I said as Mike wiped his brow. "Besides, you said you didn't really know her, so there wouldn't be attorney-client privilege."

"Why are you so interested, my little Milk Dud?" Scooter asked. "It's the guy's lunch break. Maybe he doesn't want to talk shop."

Mike patted Scooter on the back. "Yeah, I should grab something to eat.

I'll touch base later, okay?"

"Did you see the way he was sweating? It's not that hot today," I said as Mike hightailed it down Main Street toward the Sailor's Corner Cafe.

"Man, I hope he isn't coming down with something," Scooter said. "We've got the race tomorrow."

I wasn't so sure Mike was getting sick. I had a feeling my line of questioning had hit too close to home. I was pretty sure he knew more about Emily's situation than he wanted to admit to.

* * *

Later that afternoon, I successfully installed our new fuel filter and water separator unit. And I made sure everyone knew about it.

"Whoo-hoo!" I shouted from the deck of our boat. "I did it!"

Ben looked up from the thru-hull he was installing on a neighboring boat.

"That's great, Mollie. I keep telling you, you could get a job working at the boatyard if you wanted to."

"Yeah, no," I said as I climbed down the ladder. "My work for FAROUT keeps me busy enough."

"Where's Scooter? He should be here to share in your moment of triumph."

"He went to drop some paperwork off at Mike's office."

"Mike the lawyer?" I nodded. "Is it for a will?"

"No, a work contract." Ben frowned. "Why? What is it?" I asked.

"There's been some talk about Mike around town. Let's just say he operates on the edge when it comes to his law practice. He's known as the guy to go to if you want to do something shady."

"You're kidding," I said. "The last thing Scooter needs now is to have some crooked lawyer working on his stuff."

"It's just rumors," Ben said. "There might be nothing to it. What do I know about lawyers, anyway? Look at me. I'm living paycheck to paycheck. I'll never have enough money to need a lawyer, let alone hire one. I'm sorry I said anything. Let's change the subject, okay?"

"All right," I said. "Why don't you tell me about this latest T-shirt of yours."

"You like it?" he said. "I picked it up at the festival."

I took a closer look at the skull and crossbones and the slogan emblazoned underneath: "I might be the reason the rum is gone."

"It suits you," I said with a smile. "A nice addition to your pirate T-shirt collection."

As I was telling Ben about everything that had gone wrong during the installation and how many things I had to do over, Scooter pulled up in the car. "Why are you grinning from ear to ear?" he asked me.

"I did it!"

"Really, you finished already? That's great!" He stepped out of the car and pulled me into a bear hug before kissing the top of my head. "I'm so proud of my little Milk Dud. This calls for a celebration. I have just the thing." After grabbing a few bags out of the back of the vehicle, he gave me another kiss. "I'll be right back."

I spun around in a circle. "I knew it. He got me some chocolate cupcakes to celebrate!"

"Are you sure?" Ben asked. "I thought he was really serious about his diet."

"I think that particular obsession is over. These things usually last a day or two. Maybe three days tops. But he broke down and had Thai food the other night and hash browns yesterday. I think it's safe to say we can kiss Rutamentals goodbye."

Scooter climbed down the ladder with a tote bag slung over his shoulder. "I've got some good news, bad news. Which do you want first?"

"I want the one that involves chocolate."

Scooter gulped. "Sorry, neither has to do with chocolate."

"Okay, give me the bad news first."

"The fridge isn't working. But now that you're done with the fuel filter and water separator, maybe that can be the next project you tackle."

I sighed. "The good news better be extra good to make up for the fact that one more thing has broken on *Marjorie Jane*."

"I have some bubbles to celebrate. I just picked it up at the store, so it's cold." He pulled a bottle out of the bag, along with three coffee cups. Yes, coffee cups. We sure know how to celebrate in style.

"Ooh, champagne," I said. "You've outdone yourself."

"Well, it's not exactly champagne. To be champagne, it has to be—"

"Yeah, yeah, I know. It has to be made in a certain region in France. That's okay. I'm not fussy. A nice bottle of prosecco from Italy will do just fine."

"Well, it's not exactly prosecco. Here, Ben, grab these." He handed him the coffee cups, then unwrapped the foil from the top of the bottle. I wasn't sure I had heard of prosecco coming with a screw top before. What kind of bubbles were these?

After Scooter poured some into each of our cups, he made a toast. "Here's to being one step closer to sailing off into the sunset and around the world."

I choked on my drink. For two reasons, really. One, there was no way I was going to sail around the world, especially in this boat. And two, whatever was in my glass was disgusting. Even Ben seemed a little green around the gills after he took a sip, and he's the type of guy to guzzle down any kind of booze, particularly if it was free.

"What exactly is this?" I asked.

"Isn't it great?" Scooter said. He turned the bottle around so I could see the label. "It's nonalcoholic sparkling wine made out of rutabagas."

"So, I guess Rutamentals is back on," I said before downing my glass. If you can't fight them, you might as well join them.

* * *

On again, off again. Off, on. On, off. I was so confused as to what was up with Rutamentals. After choking down the Rutabubbles, Scooter announced that he was taking me to Alligator Chuck's for a celebratory dinner. Visions of ribs slathered in tangy barbecue sauce, french fries, creamy coleslaw, and a slice of brownie pie for dessert filled my head. My mouth watered. My tummy growled in anticipation. I put on a pair of shorts with some very forgiving elastic in the waistband, grabbed my purse, and hopped in the car.

Turned out Rutamentals was still on. Very much on.

Wanda had somehow convinced Chuck to serve diet-friendly meals at his restaurant. Scooter eagerly pointed out the options: rutabaga "hummus" with celery sticks, pasta made out of spiralized rutabaga and served with a creamy tofu sauce, and a rutaburger featuring plenty of rutabaga and nothing else you'd associate with a burger, like a bun, meat, or cheese.

I told Scooter to order for me and excused myself to go to the ladies' room. As I walked through the dining room, I noticed no one else had ordered anything from the Rutamentals menu. I said hi to a few people I knew, stealing some fries and nachos along the way.

On my way back from the restroom, I ran into Ned and Nancy in the entryway.

"Crowded, isn't it," Ned said. "We've been waiting almost twenty minutes for a table."

"Come join us," I offered. "We've got a booth over by the window."

"Thanks, but we're meeting our daughter, son-in-law, and the grandkids for dinner," Ned said. "Katy and Sam love coming here. I think it's the alligator hats they hand out to the kids."

"Totally understandable," I said. "Those hats are really adorable. I got one last time I was here."

Nancy snorted. "You realize those are for kids, don't you?"

"I'm not so sure about that. The waitress didn't ask to see my ID. Maybe you should get one tonight."

Nancy pursed her lips, then looked at her watch. "They're running late, as usual."

"They're only a few minutes late," Ned said. "You know how hard it is to get two young kids ready and out the door on time."

"I never had any problems with punctuality when I was raising our children." Nancy fixed Ned with a pointed stare. "Our daughter must have inherited the lateness gene from you."

While Ned stared uncomfortably at the ground, I decided to get out of there before Nancy started to analyze my DNA. I was pretty sure she'd find some unsatisfactory traits like "leaves dirty dishes in the sink overnight" and "doesn't floss regularly."

"I guess I should get back," I said. "I wouldn't want my dinner to get cold." Rutabaga was bad enough—cold rutabaga sounded dreadful.

"Hang on a sec," Ned said. "Have you heard about the funeral arrangements for Emily?"

"No. I hadn't realized the medical examiner released her body already."

"They did earlier today. Jeff stopped by the office and asked if we knew anyone who could arrange for a memorial service on a boat. He wants to scatter her ashes on the water."

"Poor guy, having to organize everything. It's a shame she didn't have any immediate family."

"You should come to the service," Ned said. "Jeff said everyone's invited."

Nancy scowled. "Why would Mollie want to go to a memorial service for someone she just met? Why would anyone?"

"Well, I'm going," Ned said firmly. "Jeff doesn't really know anyone in the area, and he could use the support. A number of people are attending. Penny, Penelope, Mike, Wanda, Norm, Alan—"

"Did you see Alan today?" Nancy asked. "He was supposed to email me the photographs from the opening weekend of the festival. I've been trying to get a hold of him all day."

"Don't worry. I mentioned it to him," Ned said.

"Good. What did he say?"

Ned scratched his head. "Well, to be honest, it was hard to tell. He mumbles at times."

"At times?" I asked. "He mumbles all the time."

"I'm not sure about that," Ned said. "He spoke pretty clearly when he heard Jeff talking about Emily's memorial service. He volunteered to come and take pictures. Jeff said he didn't need to bother, that he could take some with his phone, but Alan was very insistent."

"Well, count Scooter and me in. We'll be there to support Jeff."

"Great," Ned said. "It'll be on Friday. A sunset service. I'll let you know once I have more details."

I said my goodbyes and made my way back across the dining room, saying hello to a few more people and snagging some more fries and nachos.

"You're just in time," Scooter said as I slid into the booth. "I think you're really going to like your rutaburger."

"'Like' is such a strong word," I said before taking a bite. "Hmm. It's crunchy. I have to say, I didn't see that coming." As I placed the "burger"—and I'm using that term loosely—on my plate, I noticed Jeff and Mike sitting at a table across from us. Mike pulled a file folder out of his briefcase and handed it to Jeff. While Jeff leafed through the papers, Mike grabbed his napkin and wiped his brow. Jeff held up a document and pointed at a section, jabbing his finger repeatedly to make his point.

"I'm going to grab some ketchup," I said to Scooter. Mike and Jeff were so absorbed in their conversation that they didn't notice me leaning across the table behind them.

"Trust me," Mike said. "It'll work. All you need is a wedding certificate to take care of Emily's will. And I've got some contacts who can arrange that."

I grabbed a bottle of ketchup, and

some hot sauce for good measure, and walked back to my table, keeping my head down so the guys wouldn't notice me.

Whose wedding certificate were they talking about? And what exactly did Emily's will say? Hopefully, I would get some answers at the memorial service, if not before.

CHAPTER 9
UNICORNS VS QUADRICORNS

I woke in the morning with a vague recollection of being on a game show. Normally, dreaming of winning the grand prize would be a pleasant thing to wake up to. But in this case, it was a lifetime supply of rutabagas—the stuff of nightmares. As I rubbed the sleep out of my eyes, I resolved to be more supportive of Scooter and his dieting efforts. So I downed a Rise and Shine Smoothie with a smile on my face.

After giving my husband and Mrs.

Moto a kiss goodbye, I hopped in the car to head to the waterfront park. It was my day to staff the FAROUT booth. I was really looking forward to it. It would be a great opportunity to talk to people about other life in the universe and hopefully drum up some new members.

The bright purple awning over the Sugar Shack caught my eye as I drove down Main Street. I decided to stop and have a chat with Penelope and see if I could fill in a few blanks about the cake competition. Emily had died shortly after the first judging round with a shattered plate next to her. How did she get the plate? What kind of cake had been on it?

A cheerful tune from *The Sound of Music* caught my attention as I opened the door. Penelope peeked out from the back room. "Finally, a customer! What can I get you, Mollie?" She walked toward the counter, tucking her strawberry-blonde hair behind her ears and adjusting her purple apron. "I just took some lemon poppy seed muffins out of the oven."

I licked my lips as I gazed at the pastries in the display case. Then I took a step back and said firmly, "Thanks, but I think I'm going to have to pass."

"Wow, that's so unlike you," she said. "You must have had a big breakfast."

"You have no idea."

The door opened and two young girls ran in. "Hello, sweethearts, what can I get you?" Penelope asked.

A woman holding a baby in her arms called to them. "Girls, I told you, no cupcakes today. Come on, let's go." She gave us an apologetic smile as she shooed the kids out of the bakery.

Penelope gave a heavy sigh. "It's been like that for the past few days. People are avoiding baked goods like the plague. At this rate, I'll be out of business by the end of the week."

"But why? Everyone needs a sweet

treat from time to time."

She untied her apron and hung it up on a hook before sitting down at one of the white wrought iron tables by the window. "It's because of what happened to Emily." She put her face in her hands.

"But what does that have to do with you?"

Penelope lifted her head. Her gray eyes were damp with tears. "She was poisoned."

"But everyone knows that. It's not like people have stopped eating. There were plenty of people at Alligator Chuck's last night."

"The poison was in one of the slices of cake. And because I was a judge and run a bakery, people suspect I had something to do with it."

I reached my hand across the table and squeezed hers. "I'm sure that's not the case. It's probably that Rutamentals diet everyone is on. That's why they're avoiding sugary treats. Don't worry, it's just a fad. Soon, everyone will be sick of rutabaga and you won't be able to keep up with the demand."

Penelope wiped her eyes and smiled. "I hope you're right."

"Of course I'm right. Tell you what, why don't you get me one of those lemon poppy seed muffins and an extra-large mocha, and then we'll figure out how to get people to just say no to rutabagas and begin saying yes to sugar."

She went into the back and returned a few minutes later with two mugs and two muffins. The lemony aroma was heavenly. I dove right in while Penelope stared blankly out of the window.

After slurping down the last of my coffee and making sure there weren't any crumbs left on my plate, I asked Penelope if she knew any more about how the cake slice was poisoned.

She shook her head. "No. All Chief Dalton told me was that it *had* been poisoned, not how. He was here at the bakery questioning me for a long time yesterday."

"What kinds of questions did he ask?"

Penelope shrugged. "The usual ones, I guess—did I see anyone put anything on the cakes, where was I after Nancy locked the doors to the pavilion, did I know how Emily got back inside, what did I know about her. That kind of thing."

"And what did you say?"

"That I didn't see anything, that I didn't even know Emily, let alone who would want to murder her, and that I had been watching the fire, just like everyone else."

"Did he ask you anything else?"

"He was really interested in the bakery. He wanted to see what kind of security system I had. He even sent one of his officers to my house later to check what security I had there."

"That's odd," I said, staring forlornly at my empty cup and plate. I considered buying another muffin and coffee to support the Sugar Shack. Scooter would understand once he heard what Penelope was going through.

"I thought so too," she said. "But when I asked him about it, he said it was routine. There have been some issues with petty theft in Coconut Cove, and they're simply checking to make sure everyone has the proper precautions in place."

"Hmm. I'll have to ask him about that. There's a lot of expensive equipment at the marina. We don't need people sneaking in at night stealing it off people's boats."

A buzzer went off in the kitchen. "That's a batch of chocolate chip cookies ready to come out of the oven. Of course, no one's going to buy them," she said glumly.

"Not if I have anything to do with it. In fact, give me some of your menus. I'll pass them out at the FAROUT booth today." I looked at my phone. "In fact, I should probably get going before I'm late." No time for an extra muffin and coffee after all.

"They're right there by the cash register," she said over her shoulder as she hurried into the kitchen. "Thanks, Mollie!"

As I walked behind the counter, I noticed a framed picture of Penelope with an older woman. The two of them looked so much alike—strawberry-blonde hair, gray eyes, and cheerful smiles. It had to be a photo with her mother. I paused and took a closer look. The smile on the older woman's face didn't quite reach her eyes. *What had she been thinking about when that picture had been taken*, I wondered.

I grabbed some of the lilac-colored menus, which were wedged between a stack of plates and the cash register. That's when I realized I hadn't asked Penelope for more details about which cake had been poisoned and how Emily had gotten a hold of it. I didn't want to upset her with more questions, so I decided I'd go straight to the source for the information I needed—Chief Dalton.

* * *

"Why won't he return my calls?" I muttered under my breath.

"Who's that?" asked my former neighbor.

I gritted my teeth. Much to my dismay, I had discovered that the FAROUT booth was right next to Mrs. Moto's archenemy's art booth. I had spent the entire morning listening to her list reasons why dogs were superior to cats, why Yorkies were superior to any other breed of dog, and the health benefits of Rutamentals.

Yep, another convert to the wonders of rutabagas. She was a full-on fan of Trixie Tremblay, right down to the legwarmers she was wearing underneath her long batik skirt. She had accessorized them with ankle bracelets, which jingled every time she moved. I sighed. It felt like I had a long day ahead of me.

"Cat got your tongue?" she asked.

"If you must know, it's your ex-husband. I've been trying him all day, but he's refusing to take my call. I'd march down to the police station and demand to see him, but there's no one else available to cover the booth."

"Well, I can relate," she said. "Tiny doesn't return my calls either."

"Did you just call him Tiny?"

She smiled. "It's a nickname. I began calling him that when we first started dating. It's caught on—everyone calls him that now."

"I don't think I've ever heard anyone call him anything other than Chief Dalton."

"I guess that's true. He's not exactly

the type of guy to be on a first-name basis with many people." She rubbed her left ring finger absentmindedly. "He likes to keep people at a distance. It's one of the reasons we broke up."

"I heard it was over what you named your dogs."

"You gotta love small towns. You'd think people would have better things to do than gossip about my marriage." She held my gaze. "Or spread gossip."

My face grew warm. "I'm sorry. I shouldn't have said anything." I observed the two Yorkies sleeping in a dog bed, which she had set up for them underneath a tree. "For what it's worth, I think their names are really cute. How did you come up with them?"

"Tiny would kill me if I told you..." She hesitated for a few moments, then continued. "What the heck. It's a cute story, and it serves him right for not calling you or me back."

I leaned forward, eager to hear a

hopefully embarrassing story about the chief, but before she could dish the dirt, a couple started asking her questions about one of her paintings. While she talked to them about the techniques she used and what inspired her to depict magical creatures like fairies and leprechauns, I managed to hand out a few FAROUT brochures to college kids and some of Penelope's menus to a group of retirees.

"This calls for a celebration!" she said. "I sold one of my largest paintings. They're going to come back later and pick it up."

"Which one?"

She pointed at the back of her booth. "It's the one with the quadricorns grazing in a meadow."

"Did you say quadricorns?" I peered at the painting. "But aren't those unicorns?"

"Look closely," she said as she assembled a large, flat cardboard box.

I examined the painting in more detail. It was certainly colorful, and the use of glitter really accentuated the wildflowers. I zeroed in on the creatures in the foreground. "One, two, three, four…oh, I get it now!"

"They look like unicorns," she said as she extended a finger on the top of her head to resemble a horn. "But since they have four horns, they're called quadricorns." She giggled as she pointed four fingers upward in a perfect imitation of a four-horned unicorn. "See, a quadricorn. They're far superior to unicorns."

Her laughter was infectious, and before I knew it, I had joined in. "And people think I'm crazy for believing in extraterrestrial life," I said. "But you paint pictures of quadricorns."

"And get paid for it." She grinned. "Actually, you're not as bad as Tiny makes you out to be."

I smiled back. "And you're not as bad

as your threat to slap a restraining order on us made you out to be."

"About that—" Her watch beeped. "Time to take my pill."

"Nothing too serious, I hope."

She reached into her woven tote bag, pulled out a bottle, and washed down a pill with some rutabaga juice. "No, just something I have to take every day. I have a rare genetic condition. Runs in my family. Tiny used to remind me to take my pills every day." She held up her wrist. "Now that he's not around anymore, I have to rely on my watch."

"Speak of the devil," I said.

"Good afternoon, Mrs. McGhie," the chief said as he bent down to greet the Yorkies. He beamed as they licked his face. After giving them a good scratching, he stood, all traces of his smile disappearing in a flash as he turned to his ex-wife. "Can you look after the dogs tonight, Anabel?"

"What's come up this time?" she asked.

Remarkably, his eyebrows didn't twitch an iota, although his jaw tightened. "It's a murder investigation, Anabel. That's what's come up. And he or she is still out there, and I think they're going to strike again."

She bit her lip. "Fine. Go on. Go save the world."

He stalked off without another word while she busied herself packing up the quadricorn painting. I sat on the stool behind the FAROUT information desk in shock as I tried to make sense of what the chief had said. Who was going to be the next victim?

CHAPTER 10
LEE HO!

Fortunately, there were lots of visitors to the FAROUT booth in the afternoon, which kept me from dwelling on the chief's dire pronouncement. I passed out bumper stickers and sold some T-shirts without a care in the world.

Who was I kidding? All I could think about was figuring out who the next victim would be. I felt powerless to stop the next murder. Sure, I had a list of suspects for Emily's murder, but I had more questions than answers. As the person who'd found the poor girl's body, I felt compelled to answer those questions. There was a certain burden that came with something like that. One did have a civic responsibility, after all.

Scooter would probably say I was rationalizing things, that finding a dead body didn't mean I *had* to investigate, and that my nosiness was going to get me in trouble as it had in the past. Maybe he was right. But I couldn't help myself. And besides, my nosiness had helped nab killers in the past. I'd be doing Coconut Cove a disservice if I didn't get involved.

In between handing out brochures, signing people up for the FAROUT newsletter, and explaining the difference between carbon- and silicon-based life forms, I jotted down my "Nab the Killer, Pronto" to-do list.

1 – *Find out when the cake was poisoned.* Was it during the cake competition itself when the cakes were

being sliced, or had someone poisoned the cake after Nancy made everyone leave the pavilion? If it was the former, only the judges and the finalists had access to the cakes when they were being sliced. Everyone else was behind the barricade. And of those people, the only ones who had access to the bottle of gelsemium that was used to poison Emily were Nancy, Jeff, Mike, and Wanda. Alan was also in my line of sight. As the official event photographer, he had been allowed access behind the public barrier.

I still doubted that Nancy was a serious suspect, given how the murder had ruined her carefully organized event. She might kill someone to prevent disorganization, but she certainly wouldn't eliminate someone if it meant a disruption to her meticulously ordered life.

The other thing I had to keep in mind was that when I went around to the rear of the building in search of Mrs. Moto, the back door had been ajar. Had the murderer entered while everyone was distracted with the fire and then poisoned the cake?

2 – *Find out how the killer knew Emily would eat the deadly slice of cake.* She had been complaining loudly about how Nancy had messed up the decoration on Jeff's cake and that she wanted to fix it. Did the killer encourage her to return and replace that slice of cake, knowing that she would eat the original slice?

3 – *Figure out who wanted Emily dead and why.* Wanda and Jeff were top of my list, given their conversation about Emily outside Penelope's Sugar Shack. There were a lot of questions swirling about Jeff—what had happened to his former fiancée, his discussion of a wedding certificate and Emily's will with Mike, and what was up with his ears. Okay, that last point didn't have anything to do with the murder, but it

was still something I was very curious about.

There was definitely something suspicious about Wanda, besides the fact that she had been brainwashed by Trixie Tremblay. I realized that, although we had been taking sailing classes together for a while, I didn't actually know much about her. It wasn't until that day at the grocery store when she had become upset over the death of her sister that I had first learned something personal about her.

Mike was obviously up to his eyeballs in something dodgy. He had been nervous when I'd asked him about Emily's will, and it appeared he and Jeff were up to no good. Plus, he had written that restraining order letter, which didn't exactly put him in my or Mrs. Moto's good books.

Alan was an interesting suspect. He was so meek and mild that I couldn't see him being the killer, let alone imagine what would drive him to murder a young woman like Emily. But he was a strange little man, and those were often the ones you had to watch out for.

I looked over at Anabel in the booth next to me. Part of me really liked her. She was an incredible artist, she didn't mock my involvement in FAROUT, and she had a good sense of humor. But the other part of me was still annoyed. I flipped over the page in my notebook and began another list of questions:

1 – What did Anabel have against Mrs. Moto?

2 – What was the story behind the chief's nickname, Tiny?

3 – If there were unicorns and quadricorns, were there also unicorns with two or three horns?

After I got that out of my system, I flipped back to my "Nab the Killer, Pronto" list and thought about the most important thing that I needed to investigate—who was the killer going after next? My fear was that the murderer believed someone had seen him or her poison the cake during the competition and wanted to eliminate any witnesses. I knew from watching my favorite television show that was what murderers did—made sure no one was left alive who could identify them.

I had been right there in the thick of things. Could the murderer have thought I had seen something I shouldn't have? Maybe there was something to be said for avoiding sugary treats, which might potentially be laced with poison. Or was it possible this was all Trixie Tremblay's doing somehow? The cake poisoning might have driven people to embrace Rutamentals. You can never be too careful about people who have an unnatural obsession with root vegetables.

I snapped my notebook shut and shoved it in my bag. It was time to head to the Palm Tree Marina for the sailing race. I was excited and nervous at the same time. Excited to participate in my first sailing race ever and nervous that the killer might think it was the perfect opportunity to go after his or her next victim. Pushing someone overboard might go unnoticed during the excitement of the race. I was planning on staying sharp. No one was going overboard on the ocean on my watch.

* * *

When I got to the marina, everything was in full swing. Crews were busy getting the boats ready for the race— taking off the sail covers, making sure everything was battened down, and checking equipment. As I walked down the creaky dock, I kept a sharp lookout for sea monsters. The last thing I wanted was to trip on one of the loose planks, fall into the water, and get eaten by a kraken.

"There you are!" Penny was standing on the bow of her boat, *Pretty in Pink*.

"Sorry," I said as I climbed on board. "The volunteer who was taking over for me at the FAROUT booth was late."

"Quick, change into the team T-shirt down below," she said, pulling a pale-pink shirt out of a bag.

"These turned out great," I said. "I love how you've got the breast cancer ribbon on the back."

"Well, if we win—and we are going to win—then I've earmarked the money that was raised to be donated to breast cancer research." She pointed at Norm, who was standing on the deck of his boat posing for pictures. "Guess what Norm is going to donate the money to if he wins."

"Himself?"

"Yep, his campaign fund."

"Well, even more reason for us to win," I said, giving her a fist bump.

Wanda tossed a coiled rope into the

cockpit. "How come you haven't changed yet?" Penny asked her.

I looked at the teal T-shirt Wanda was wearing. Surprise, surprise. It featured Trixie Tremblay holding a purple plate laden with sliced rutabaga. Yellow legwarmers and deck shoes completed the outfit.

"I wish I could, but I can't. I'm contractually obligated to wear Trixie Tremblay gear."

"Great, now we have an extra T-shirt." Penny threw up her hands. "So much for a matching all-female crew."

After checking that all the preparations were in order, she looked at the checklist that Nancy had given her. "Just one thing left to do—have Alan take an official crew photograph." She turned to me. "Mollie, would you mind getting him so we can get this over with and head out toward the starting line? I see him over by Mike's boat."

"Sure," I said. "That way I can give

Scooter a good-luck kiss before the race starts."

As I walked down the dock toward *Naut Guilty*, I noticed Jeff towering over Alan. He attempted to grab Alan's camera, but the mousy man pulled back, almost falling into the water before he caught himself on one of the wooden pilings.

"Delete them," Jeff hissed.

"I'm telling you, I don't have any on this card," Alan said. "They're all saved on the cloud."

"So you admit it, you do have photos of her!"

Alan stepped forward and jabbed his finger in Jeff's chest. "She wanted me to take them. They're all I have left of her, and I'm sure as heck not going to delete them!" he said, clearly enunciating every word. I was stunned—the mouse had turned into a lion.

Jeff shoved Alan's hand down, then put his arm around his shoulders.

"Listen, mate. I understand. She was a pretty girl, but you have to admit it's a bit creepy that you've got photos of her."

"She was my girlfriend," Alan said quietly.

Jeff slapped Alan's back. "Hardly, mate. She went on a few pity dates with you, that's all."

"It wasn't pity." His eyes looked flinty as he stared up at Jeff. "Emily was interested in me and my work."

"Your work, maybe, but not you." Jeff shrugged. "Tell you what, go ahead and keep the photos. No skin off my back. After all, I'm the one she was in love with. There was a ring on her finger to prove it." He gave Alan one more hearty slap on the back. "I better get back to the boat. See you around."

As Jeff walked toward me, I tried to remember which of his ears had seemed bigger than the other. The sun was reflecting off the water, making it hard to get a view of the left side of his face.

"You okay, Mollie?" Jeff cocked his head toward me. Ah. It was definitely his left ear that was oddly shaped.

"Me? I'm fine. It's Alan I'm worried about. Is he okay?" I asked, noting how the photographer was digging his fingers into the palms of his hands.

"Just girl problems," Jeff said with a laugh. "Good thing you're married, or he might try to ask you out. Gotta go help get the boat ready. It's going to be sweet when we cross the finish line and win this thing."

"In your dreams," I said over my shoulder. After getting Alan's attention, I explained about needing him to take the *Pretty in Pink* crew picture. He avoided eye contact with me and mumbled a response. "Do you mind speaking up a little?" I asked gently.

"I'll be right there," he said more clearly. "I'm also going to take a video."

"Oh my gosh, a video! I completely

forgot that you videoed the cake competition." Alan nodded. "Can I see a copy of the footage you took? Is it on this camera?" This could be the key to finding out who put the poison on the cake. It wouldn't be the first time that a video of Alan's had provided an important clue in one of my investigations.

"The police seized the camera I used that day," he said. Darn. Not much chance that the chief was going to let me see the key piece of evidence. Then he added, "But it automatically backs up to the cloud."

"Ooh. Would I be able to access it?" I asked, rubbing my hands together. Thank goodness for the magical cloud.

"I suppose, if…" His voice trailed off as he shuffled his feet on the dock.

"If what?"

"If you convince Penny to let me come on her boat during the race and take pictures."

"Well, it's supposed to be an all-female crew." Alan surprised me by making eye contact with me for a few seconds. It was unnerving. I quickly looked away. "But I guess I could persuade her." As we walked toward *Pretty in Pink*, I remembered the extra T-shirt. "How do you feel about wearing pink?"

* * *

As *Pretty in Pink* tacked along on the starting line waiting for the race to begin, I looked nervously at the boat Scooter was crewing on, *Naut Guilty*. Mike and Jeff were aboard that boat, and one of them might be the murderer. Then I glanced around the boat I was on, my eyes resting on Wanda in her Trixie Tremblay getup and Alan clad in the spare pink shirt. The killer could potentially be here as well. I wrapped my arms around me, shivering despite the warm weather.

The starting gun sounded, jarring me out of my thoughts. "Come on, people, let's go!" Penny cheered from the helm. She steered the boat toward the first mark while the crew focused on trimming the sails. At that moment, we were all seated on the port side, our weight helping to balance the boat.

"Ready about," Penny said.

Two of the women shifted to the starboard side, while Wanda and I stayed on the port side. "Ready," we all said in unison.

As Penny turned the boat, we pulled and released the lines, causing the headsail to shift effortlessly from one side of the boat to the other. We executed a flawless tack, putting *Pretty in Pink* in the lead.

Hang on. I should probably stop here and point something out. Did you notice all that technical babble I uttered? It sounded like I actually knew what I was doing when it came to sailing, didn't it? And like we were a superb crew? Well, let's just say that's not exactly how it happened. Here's how it really went down.

"Ready about," Penny said.

The woman on my right looked at me and frowned. "I forgot what we're supposed to do."

"What's going on, ladies?" Penny asked. She tapped her fingers on the steering wheel. "Come on, get it together. You've done this a million times in practice. Mollie, Wanda, over to the starboard side. Now!"

As Wanda and I rose, a wave crashed into the side of the boat, jostling us. "Ouch," Wanda said. "You hit my head."

"You hit my shoulder."

"Ladies," Penny said. "If we don't tack soon, we're going to hit that reef over there." She took a deep breath. "Ready about?"

"Ready," we all said in unison.

"Meow," someone else said.

I looked at the companionway. Alan was standing on the ladder, which led down to the cabin below, taking photos of us in all our incompetent glory. Perched next to him was Mrs. Moto.

"How did that cat get on board?" Penny said. "Never mind, we'll deal with that in a minute. Lee ho!"

While she turned the boat into the wind, we pulled and released the lines, shifting the sail awkwardly from one side of the boat to the other. In the process, Wanda tangled her foot up in a line on the cockpit floor. As I tried to unwrap it from her legwarmer, I fell off the bench. Mrs. Moto ran over to me, meowed loudly, then licked my face.

"Mollie, get that cat down below. Lock her in the V-berth."

"She's not going to like that," I said.

"I don't care what she likes. She's going to get herself killed running around loose."

I grabbed the cat and hustled down below. "How exactly did you get onto Penny's boat?" Mrs. Moto responded with a loud purr. I smiled. She looked adorable snuggled up in my arms. "You're going to have to stop getting into places where people don't want you. You don't want another restraining order, do you?"

I set her on one of the cushions in the V-berth and quickly closed the door. Not a second later, the yowling started. "Shush," I said. "If you're quiet, I'll give you some extra catnip when we get home." I paused for a minute and listened. No yowling, just a soft meow.

"All right, ladies, we're going to tack again in a few minutes," Penny said. "We can do this. Just remember your training. And don't forget that it's for a good cause—fighting breast cancer and beating the guys."

I'm pleased to report that after that disastrous first tack, we got our act together and took the lead. The two boats trailing us—*Naut Guilty* and Norm's boat *The Codfather II*—didn't have a chance of catching up to us. After making it around the last mark, we headed into the home stretch. I couldn't believe it—we were going to win this thing!

"What is he doing?" Wanda yelled. We all turned and looked behind us. *The Codfather II* was on a collision course with *Naut Guilty*.

"Turn, turn," Penny said, staring at *The Codfather II* as it closed in on the other boat. "Norm, for goodness' sake, turn!"

Norm turned, but it was too late. I flinched as the bow of his boat slammed into the side of *Naut Guilty*.

"Scooter!" I yelled. Mrs. Moto joined in with a piercing cry, which could be heard all the way up in the cockpit. I gripped Penny's arm. "Are they going to be okay?"

"They'll be fine. See that boat over there?" She pointed at a small powerboat speeding toward the accident scene. "They're trained to handle situations like this. The best thing we can do is hold our position here until they give the all clear. If we try to go and help, we'll just get in the way and make things worse."

She comforted me while we waited for news. "Do you want Mrs. Moto to come up here so you can give her a cuddle?" Penny asked. I nodded. "Will one of you ladies go get her?"

Wanda volunteered. When she handed me the upset calico, I noticed that Mrs. Moto had shed a lot of hair on Trixie Tremblay's face. Then it hit me. I knew who the murderer's next victim was going to be.

CHAPTER 11
COCONUT CARL

"Hey, take it easy," Scooter said as I embraced him. "You're squeezing the stuffing out of me."

I stepped back and stared into his dark-brown puppy-dog eyes. "Sorry, you're not going to get off that easy. I thought I had lost you when the boats collided. I need at least one more hug."

He chuckled as he pulled me into his arms. "I'm okay," he whispered into my ear before giving me a kiss. A piercing yowl interrupted our tender moment.

"I'm not the only one who needs some reassurance," I said.

Scooter scooped up Mrs. Moto and gave her a cuddle. "I heard you went racing," he said to the calico. "The first feline member of the *Pretty in Pink* crew. I hope you got a T-shirt."

I smiled at the thought of her sporting a cat-sized pink top. After stroking her head, I gave Scooter an appraising look. "Are you sure you're okay?"

"Absolutely fine. Not even a scratch." Unfortunately, the same couldn't be said for everyone else. One of the crew members on *The Codfather II* had broken an arm, and a couple of guys on *Naut Guilty* had some pretty serious cuts, bumps, and bruises.

Both boats had limped back to the marina after the injured men had been taken off by the rescue boat. The paint on *Naut Guilty*'s hull was scraped off where *The Codfather II* had smashed into her, and the fiberglass underneath was in bad shape. The deck was even worse. *The Codfather II* had suffered serious damage as well—her bowsprit had been torn off, her forestay had been detached, and her mast was hanging at a precarious angle. Even if you didn't know what a bowsprit and forestay were, one look at the sailboat would have been enough to convince you that there was going to be a hefty repair bill.

The uninjured crew members and race spectators had gathered at the marina patio. Everyone was buzzing about what had happened and who was to blame. The crowd was divided into two camps —those who thought Norm was a reckless skipper and those who thought he had just done what it took to win the race and admired him for it. Norm, of course, was basking in the attention, posing for photographs and signing people up for his campaign mailing list.

In contrast, Mike was pacing back and forth along the boardwalk, his phone pressed against his ear. "I wonder what's going on," I said.

"I think he's talking to his insurance agent," Scooter said. "It's going to cost a pretty penny to fix his boat." He set Mrs. Moto on the ground. "Everyone is heading over to the Tipsy Pirate for the awards ceremony."

"Is that still on? They halted the race when the accident happened." I rubbed my temples. I could feel a headache coming on. My lack of sleep was catching up with me. "Did you know that some folks are actually complaining that the race was stopped? Apparently, *real* racers don't stop for anything."

"I guess they do things differently in Coconut Cove." He shrugged. "In any case, the skippers and the judges talked it over, and they decided to go ahead with the event. Although there won't be prizes for the race, they don't want the catering to go to waste." He looked around the patio. "Besides, I have a feeling people are going to want to keep dissecting what happened over a few drinks. To be honest, I could use a gin and tonic."

"Tell you what—why don't you take Mrs. Moto back to the boat and meet me back here. I've got something I need to take care of first."

"I'm afraid to ask."

"Don't worry, I'll fill you in later. I think you're going to want to have that drink first."

* * *

After Scooter and Mrs. Moto headed toward the boatyard, our wandering feline firmly clipped into her harness and leash, I made a beeline for Chief Dalton. He was sitting at one of the patio tables, his back toward me, intently focused on something in front of him. As I approached, I caught a glimpse of a certificate of some kind. Perhaps a birth certificate? It was too hard to see over the burly man's shoulder. He flipped the piece of paper over.

"What can I do for you, Mrs. McGhie?" he asked without turning around.

"How did you know it was me?"

"You have a distinctive walk."

I looked down at my feet. "I'm wearing flip-flops. Everyone wears flip-flops in Florida. They all make the same sound —flip, flop. How is my 'flip, flop' any different from anyone else's?"

"No comment."

Great. We were back to his non-response responses. I pulled out a chair and sat next to him. I drummed my fingers on the table.

"Is there something you wanted to say?"

I took a deep breath. "Yes, but only if you promise me something first."

He raised one of his bushy eyebrows. "That isn't how this works."

"Fine. We'll play your little game," I

said. "This is too important." I paused for a few moments to collect my thoughts.

"Well?" he prompted.

"I know who the murderer is going to go after next." There was absolutely no response, not even a 'no comment.' I leaned across the table. "Aren't you even the slightest bit curious?"

"I'm always interested to hear your theories." There was a distinct lack of conviction in his voice.

I had hoped for some sort of drum roll. Instead, there was just the sound of coconuts falling from the palm trees onto the patio. "It's Penelope. The killer was after her, not Emily."

"And why do you think that?"

"Remember how there was a broken plate by Emily's body? It was purple. I had completely forgotten until this afternoon on *Pretty in Pink*. Wanda was wearing one of those awful Trixie Tremblay T-shirts. You're not one of those wackos on the Rutamentals diet, are you?"

"This has something to do with rutabagas?"

"Yes. I mean, no. I mean, yes." I put my head in my hands. Everything was getting so jumbled up. It was probably the stress from the accident coupled with the fact that I hadn't had any real food in hours. Scooter had mentioned catering at the Tipsy Pirate. I wondered what they were going to serve. The chef there made these amazing egg rolls with a pineapple dipping sauce.

"Earth to Mrs. McGhie. So which is it —yes or no?"

I popped a breath mint in my mouth to quiet my stomach. "No, the murder doesn't have anything to do with rutabagas. At least I don't think it did. Although, that is an interesting idea—"

"I don't have all day."

"On Wanda's T-shirt, Trixie Tremblay was holding a purple plate with sliced rutabaga. That's how I made the connection. Each of the judges had a different-colored plate at the cake competition. Nancy announced what color each judge was assigned. Penelope was purple. I think the killer was trying to poison Penelope, and somehow, by mistake, Emily ended up eating the slice of cake instead. That means I've been going about my investigation all wrong."

"Your investigation?" the chief asked dryly.

"Okay, fine. Our investigation."

He smiled faintly. "Ours?"

"You know, this would work so much better if you were more of a team player. If it wasn't for my help in the other murder investigations, the killers would have gotten off scot-free."

"I see."

I shook my head. "This isn't getting us anywhere. What you really need to do is make sure that Penelope is okay. Who knows when the murderer is going to strike again."

"You don't need to worry about Miss Pringle."

I leaned back in my chair. Something was off. It was almost like... "Wait a minute. You already knew about Penelope, didn't you?"

"No co—"

I held up my hands. "Yeah, yeah. I know what you're going to say—'No comment.' Just at least promise me that she's okay."

After a beat, he said gently, "She'll be fine. My officers are watching her around the clock." Then he placed the papers in front of him in a folder, pushed back his chair, and stood. "This is why you should leave murder investigations to the professionals. We have the training and the resources required. You have a vivid imagination and a...um... cat."

I tucked my frizzy hair behind my ears. Maybe I should just keep out of it. After all, I'd had it all wrong. Emily hadn't been the intended victim. My suspect list was useless. The investigation had been a waste of time. I chewed on my lip. Maybe the chief was right. But he didn't have to make me feel so stupid about it.

"By the way, what was it you wanted me to promise?" he asked.

I gave him a calculating look. "To tell me how you got the nickname Tiny."

His face reddened while his eyebrows did the most amazing contortions. He spluttered. "What exactly did my wife—I mean my ex-wife—say to you?"

"No comment," I said, smiling sweetly.

* * *

After my disastrous conversation with the chief, I checked my messages. Scooter had texted to say that he'd been delayed. Apparently, one can of Frisky Feline Ocean's Delight hadn't been enough to satisfy our princess, and he was hunting in the cupboards trying to find some more.

My mom had also finally texted back. *Do you still see Mary?* I was even more confused than ever. How could I still see a twin sister I hadn't known about until recently? I didn't even bother to text back. This was probably best handled in a phone conversation. But after everything that had happened, I wasn't up to dealing with it at the moment.

I looked over at Mike. He kept pacing back and forth, talking on his phone. Except for the two of us, the patio was deserted. The crowd had moved the party to the Tipsy Pirate. I was eager to get there as well. Given my run of luck lately, I wanted to pay a visit to my buddy, Coconut Carl, and see if he had any advice for me.

Mike's call must have ended badly. He uttered some very imaginative expletives, then looked like he was going to hurl his phone across the patio before he stopped himself.

"Everything okay?" I asked.

"No, everything is *not* okay!" He ran his fingers through his hair. "I'm sorry. I shouldn't be taking it out on you."

"What's going on?"

"It turns out my boat wasn't insured for racing. That's something extra you have to add on to your policy."

"What about Norm? He hit your boat. Doesn't he have to pay to repair yours?"

"That's how it should work, but Norm is claiming that I was at fault. By now, I bet he's bribed everyone to tell his version of the story."

"Can't you fight it? Maybe sue him? Being a lawyer has got to count for something."

He clenched his fists. "Suing him would take time. And I don't have time. I need that money now. I need to get it from him one way or another." He slowly uncurled his fingers, then stuck his hands in his pockets. "How could I have been so stupid about the insurance?"

"I know what you mean about feeling stupid," I said.

"Do you and Scooter have problems with your boat insurance too?"

"No. At least I don't think we do." I mentally added 'check insurance' to my *Marjorie Jane* to-do list. I would say that our boat's to-do list was growing longer by the day, but it seemed more like by the hour.

"So what do you feel stupid about?"

I weighed up whether to tell him about Penelope having been the murderer's real target. Mike had been nervous when I'd questioned him about Emily's will, but, in hindsight, that didn't have anything to do with her death, since she wasn't the person who was supposed to have been killed. Maybe he had been nervous for another reason. Given his odd conversation with Jeff about a wedding certificate, I still wondered if he was engaging in some less-than-legitimate activities, but that really wasn't my business.

Since the chief had admitted that Penelope was under police protection, I figured it was already common knowledge—or would be soon—so I decided to fill Mike in. After I had explained about the purple plate, Mike frowned. "That changes everything." He pulled his phone out of his pocket. "Hang on a sec. I need to send a quick text."

"Who do you think would want to kill Penelope?" I asked. "I can't imagine anyone having it in for her. She owns a bakery, after all."

"You're right. It wouldn't make sense to eliminate Coconut Cove's source of cupcakes and cookies," Mike said with a teasing tone to his voice.

I smiled. "I like a man who thinks logically."

"I have to admit to having a certain

fondness for her vanilla spice cupcakes. My waistline hasn't been the same since she opened the Sugar Shack."

"When was that?"

"Hmm, let me think." Mike leaned against the railing and gazed out at the water for a few moments. "About four years ago? It was after she graduated from college and moved back to Coconut Cove."

"You must know her pretty well," I said. "You've lived in Coconut Cove all your life, haven't you?"

He shrugged. "I don't know about pretty well. But it is a small town, so we do keep tabs on one another. It's both a blessing and a curse." He glanced at his phone when it beeped, then turned to me with a thoughtful look on his face. "You were asking who might have it in for Penelope. There's one person I can think of that the police should be talking to."

"Who's that?"

"Wanda. She and Penelope's mom didn't speak to each other. In fact, they'd go out of their way to cross the street if they saw the other one on the same side. Wanda used to say some horrible things about Penelope's mom. Really horrible things. Maybe the bad blood extended toward her daughter."

"You think she would have killed Penelope because she didn't like her mother?"

He wiped his brow. "It's just a theory. But there's always been some questions about the circumstances surrounding the death of Penelope's mom." His phone beeped again. "Listen, I've got to go."

Wow. That left me with a lot to think about. Could Wanda be a killer? Then I shook my head. It wasn't my business. I made a vow to leave things to the police and instead focus on more important things like dinner.

* * *

"Come on, just do it. Rub his belly," I said. "We could use some good luck."

"What? Rub whose belly?" Scooter asked.

"Duh. Carl's."

"I'm not rubbing any strange guy's belly."

"But you know Carl."

"I do? Are you sure? I can't think of anybody named Carl that I know. Unless you're talking about Carl Kowalski, but he's back in Cleveland."

"No, not that Carl. *That* Carl." I pointed at the wooden statue of Coconut Carl that graced the entryway of the Tipsy Pirate. Coconut Carl was a legend in these parts. A pirate by trade and a womanizer in his spare time, Carl was known for his love of rum and coconuts. Locals and tourists alike believed it was good luck to drink a shot of rum, then rub the statue's belly three times.

Scooter shook his head. "Do you know how many people have had their hands on there?" We watched as a couple of the guys who had been on Mike's boat demonstrated the ritual. One of the guys even kissed Carl's belly. I suspected that more than one shot of rum might have been involved. "I've got enough to worry about without catching a cold or the flu by touching that."

"I've got disinfectant wipes in my bag."

"I'm sure my little Milk Dud does." He grabbed my elbow and steered me into the bar. "You've got everything in there —your phone, wallet, at least three notebooks, a ridiculous number of pens, chocolate—"

"I'm actually out of chocolate."

Scooter smiled. "I'm stunned."

"Me too. It's almost like someone went into my bag and threw it out." I gave him a playful punch in the arm.

"The nerve of some people." He rubbed his arm. "Now, where should we sit—at the *Pretty in Pink* table or the *Naut Guilty* table?"

"It's not a very good turnout at the *Naut Guilty* table," I said. Mike was conspicuously absent, and the folks with injuries were home recuperating. "Why don't we get the guys who are here to join the girls at the *Pretty in Pink* table?"

"Good idea."

While Scooter organized moving tables and chairs, I sat next to Wanda and placed an order. Thankfully, she had changed her outfit since the race. I don't think I could have managed to look at Trixie Tremblay holding a purple plate all night.

"So, what did we miss?" I asked.

"Norm just gave a speech," Wanda said.

"Can't say I'm sorry about missing that."

"I don't blame you." She took a sip of her drink. "Any word on the injured guys?"

"They're all going to be fine, even the one with the broken arm. It was a clean break."

"I broke my leg once," Wanda said wistfully. "My sister was pregnant at the time, really far along. We used to joke about who took longer to get up off the couch. I was such a klutz with my crutches, and she struggled to hoist herself up unaided. It was easier to ring a bell and have my brother-in-law fetch things for us when we needed them."

"That was sweet of him."

"Sweet...no, he wasn't sweet. Manipulative, yes. Sweet, no." She twisted the bracelet on her wrist while she stared out the large windows that overlooked the bay. "You know, I'm actually really tired. It's been a long day, and I've got food demonstrations early tomorrow at the grocery store. I'm going to call it a night."

"Where's Wanda dashing off to?"

I looked up. Nancy was standing next

to the empty chair holding a clipboard. "I'm not sure. One minute she was talking about her sister and brother-in-law, the next minute she was gone."

"She talked to you about her family?" She peered at me over her reading glasses. "Wanda never talks about her past. Her life before Coconut Cove is a mystery. All we know is that she was originally from Destiny Key."

"Destiny Key? Isn't that where Emily was from?"

"I believe so." Nancy sat down. "It's a strange place. The folks who live there are a tight-knit group who have a lot of money. They don't like outsiders visiting their island."

"But it's not a private island, is it?"

"No, but the locals resent visitors. There's a beautiful anchorage there that people from Coconut Cove sail up to. Folks take their dinghies to the beach, but if you walk anywhere else on the island, you're made to feel unwelcome pretty quickly."

"I wonder how Jeff met Emily," I said as the waitress set my drink down, along with some egg rolls. Nancy snatched one up, dipping it into the pineapple sauce and into her mouth before I had a chance to pull the plate toward me. "If they don't like outsiders, I wonder what they thought about her being engaged to one."

"I guess it will have to remain an unsolved mystery, now that the poor girl is dead." She grabbed another egg roll, along with her clipboard. "I better get back to my rounds. You're all set for the pet-costume competition, aren't you? You've read the rules and regulations, correct?"

I nodded while I savored my egg roll.

"Your costume is fully compliant?"

I dabbed my mouth with a napkin. "Um…compliant?"

She frowned while jotting down a note. "Noncompliant costumes will be automatically disqualified. You might want to reread those rules and regulations."

"I'll do that." While I ate another egg roll, I tried to remember if I had turned those particular rules and regulations into origami birds. Then I noticed Jeff and Mike at the bar looking thick as thieves. They both glanced over in my direction. Mike held up his glass and toasted me before leaning toward Jeff and whispering something in his ear. I had a feeling my investigation was back on.

CHAPTER 12
RUTABAGA POISONING

"I'm pretty sure rutabagas go bad if they're not refrigerated," I said to Ben. "Since our fridge is broken, that means I should probably throw away all the Rutamentals diet food Scooter has on board our boat, right?"

Ben scratched his head. "Uh, aren't rutabagas a root vegetable like potatoes and yams? You don't need to keep those chilled, so you shouldn't need to worry about your rutabagas going bad."

"I thought I could count on you for

support," I said. "Now repeat after me: you can get food poisoning from eating rutabagas that haven't been kept below forty degrees Fahrenheit. That's what we're going to tell Scooter, okay?"

After Ben managed to recite the food-safety mantra correctly without breaking into laughter, we sat in the folding chairs underneath *Marjorie Jane* to take a break from boat work. Ben had been helping take the mast off *The Codfather II* with the aid of a crane, while I had been trying to troubleshoot why our fridge wasn't working. After the accident at the sailing race the previous day, I was having a hard time focusing on that particular project.

I scooched my chair back a few inches to try to get in the shade, then grimaced as I took a sip of warm water. What I wouldn't have given for a cold drink. I had just about gotten used to not having a freezer since we moved onto our boat, but not having a fridge was quickly getting very tiresome.

"Isn't that Scooter pulling in now?" Ben asked. "There goes your opportunity to throw out the rutabaga food items before he got back."

"Great. It was going to be the most productive thing I did today. I might as well give up now and take a nap."

"Come on, it can't be that bad," he said after taking a sip of his icy-cold soda. I was tempted to see if he'd sell the rest of it to me, but I was feeling too lazy to climb up the ladder onto my boat and dig through my purse to find some money. Warm water it was.

Scooter pulled up one of the other chairs and sat next to me. "Did you get the fridge working?" he asked.

"No," I said. "Either something's wrong with the compressor, or we need to add more magic gas to it."

"Magic gas?" Scooter asked with a puzzled look on his face. "What's that?"

Ben grinned like a five-year-old boy.

"Sounds like unicorn farts. It probably has glitter in it."

"Hmm. I'll have to ask Anabel Dalton about that," I said. "She's the town expert on unicorns and quadricorns."

"Uh, quadricorns," Scooter said. "Let's get back to that in a minute. First, can you tell me what this 'magic gas' is all about? Is fixing our fridge going to be expensive?"

"It's a substance that starts off as a gas, then goes through the compressor, turns into a liquid, then finally goes through the evaporator and turns back to a gas, and, in the process, magically keeps everything in your fridge cool."

Scooter smiled. "I have no idea what you just said, but you're awfully cute when you talk about marine technical stuff."

"I think she's talking about adding some refrigerant to your system," Ben said. "Kind of like topping up your car's air-conditioning system. It comes in a can. You can pick it up at Melvin's."

"Bingo," I said. "One of the guys a couple of boats over told me about it. He offered to help if that turns out to be the issue."

"I still can't get over how you know this," Scooter said. "For someone who didn't want to own a sailboat, let alone work on fixing one up, you've sure become pretty knowledgeable about it all. I think you know more than I do."

"I'm just as surprised as you are," I said. "It does make me wonder if I've been abducted by aliens and if they did something funny to my brain. Do you realize I actually read a whole chapter on fixing marine refrigeration systems in that boring boat-repair book we have?"

"Is that the one Mrs. Moto likes sleeping on?" Scooter asked.

"Yep, that's the one. She's really taken to napping on books these days. Doesn't matter what kind of book it is, she just curls up on top and begins snoozing away."

"Not just on closed books," Scooter said. "I saw her nudge one open yesterday with her nose. She flipped the pages over until she found just the right section, then settled down on top of the open book."

"Where is Mrs. Moto?" Ben asked.

"She's napping inside in the air conditioning. Unlike us foolish humans sitting outside sweltering in the heat."

"Why don't you go take a nap?" Scooter asked.

"I'd like to, but what I really need to do is finish the alterations to Mrs. Moto's costume."

"What's she dressing up as?" Ben asked.

"It's a surprise. You'll have to wait until Sunday to see." With the cake contest having ended on a disastrous note, I was pinning all my hopes on winning the pet-costume competition. I already had a place picked out on the boat to put the trophy—on a shelf above the chart table. Of course, I'd have to move Scooter's new collection of Rutamentals cookbooks to make room, but I was sure he would understand.

"What is today, anyway?" Ben asked. "I've lost track of what day of the week it is."

"Did you have one too many at the Tipsy Pirate last night?" Scooter asked.

"Well, maybe," Ben said sheepishly. "There was this really cute girl sitting at the bar watching my band play. I was trying to get up the nerve to go talk to her during a break, but then this other guy swooped in, started chatting her up, and I lost the opportunity. My buddy bought a few rounds of shots to try to cheer me up."

Poor Ben. He never seemed to have any luck with the ladies. I tried to think of any women I knew who would be interested in a sweet guy who lived on a sailboat. The problem was that there weren't many of them out there. It seemed like unattached male sailors outnumbered female ones by leaps and bounds.

"I know what you're doing," Scooter whispered to me. "You're trying to think about who you can fix him up with. I think you should stay out of it. Remember the last time you tried to set someone up?" In a louder voice, he said to Ben, "It's Wednesday."

"Yeah, that makes sense," Ben said. "Another week whizzing by."

"That's probably because so much has happened. The festival opened on Saturday and…" My voice trailed off as I thought about the drama that had ensued on Saturday with Emily's death and all that had transpired since then. I couldn't believe it was only Wednesday. Hopefully, we could make it through to the close of the festival on Sunday without another murder.

"What were you going to say?" Ben

prompted.

"I don't know. Just thinking about Emily, I guess. Has anyone heard anything about her memorial service?"

"Ned emailed the marina staff," Ben said, pulling his phone out of his pocket. "Here it is. The service is going to be on Friday evening. Jeff's chartered a boat so he can scatter her ashes at sea while the sun is setting."

"I like that idea," Scooter said. "That's what I want you to do—take *Marjorie Jane* out at sunset and scatter my ashes."

"Don't talk like that," I said. "I don't want to think about you dying."

"I don't want to think about it either for a long, long time. That's the point of Rutamentals. Eating better so we can live longer."

"Speaking of Rutamentals, Ben was telling me that you can get food poisoning from eating rutabagas that haven't been refrigerated. Isn't that right, Ben?"

"I'm not sure I'm the best person to ask. I can barely remember what day of the week it is," he replied.

"Nicely dodged," I said, punching him in the arm.

"I thought so too." Ben smiled. "Ned also attached a copy of Emily's obituary. Want me to read it out loud?"

"Sure," I said, taking a swig of my very warm water before passing the bottle to Scooter.

"Emily van der Byl, aged twenty-nine, lifelong resident of Destiny Key, passed away in Coconut Cove on—"

Scooter leaned forward. "Did you say Emily van der Byl?"

"Didn't I pronounce it correctly?" Ben asked.

"I think so," Scooter said. "It's not a very common name. I only know one other person with that name, or rather *knew* one other person—Maarten van der Byl."

"Who's that?" I asked.

"You know that contract dispute I have going on? It's with his company."

"That's odd," I said. "What are the chances of knowing two people with an unusual last name like that?" I turned to Ben. "Does it say anything about her family in the obituary?"

Ben scrolled down. "Yes. It says that she was predeceased by her mother, Laura van der Byl, and her father, Maarten van der Byl. No mention of any other relatives."

Scooter rubbed his temples. "I wish I had known who she was. Maybe I could have spoken with her directly about the contract issues."

"You're assuming she had inherited her father's business," I said.

"That's my understanding. My lawyer mentioned that Maarten van der Byl's daughter took over after his death. That's when we started having issues. They're trying to change all the terms and conditions, payment schedules, intellectual property agreements— everything. They've got so much money that I'm afraid they'll tie us up in court for years, and I'll end up broke in the process."

I tried to reconcile the Emily I had met —a sweet young woman who seemed more interested in fashion than accounting—with a cutthroat business owner out to destroy my husband's livelihood. It was like there had been two different personalities inside her. I thought about this for a moment. Had there been two different personalities or two different people? Had someone else been calling the shots when it came to the Van der Byl business?

* * *

After the revelations about Emily van der Byl and her father, Scooter got a headache. I gave him a couple of pain relievers and suggested he lie down for a while. Mrs. Moto was in a feisty mood, running back and forth across the boat batting her origami birds, which wasn't doing Scooter's headache much good. So I grabbed my cat and her costume and headed to the marina lounge to work on the alterations in order to give my husband some peace and quiet.

"Stop wiggling," I said to the squirming ball of fur on the couch. "I just need to put this one pin in, and I don't want to stick you with it." After aligning the zipper against the seam and fastening it in place, I pulled the costume over her head and freed her from my grasp. She darted across the room and leaped onto the bookshelf, perching next to a stack of books.

"Don't give me that look. You're the one who wanted to wear this particular outfit. I gave you two options—you coughed up a hairball on the other one and started kneading this one while purring. Your choice was clear. If you want to look your best, then we need to make sure the bottom part fits just right."

Mrs. Moto's response was to knock one of the books onto the floor, then begin washing behind her ears. After folding her costume and setting it on the coffee table, I picked the book up. "Oh, good choice," I said. "I've read this one. Do you want to know whodunit?" I took her loud yowl to be an affirmative. "It was the butler. I know that's a cliché, but in this case, it really was the butler."

After I placed the mystery back on the shelf, she knocked another one down. "This one was trickier," I said as I leafed through the pages. "I thought I knew who the murderer was, but the author had a huge twist at the end. I didn't see it coming."

Another book landed at my feet. "You're really enjoying this game, aren't you?" I asked. A pair of green eyes stared down at me innocently. "Okay, I have to admit, I didn't love this one. The characters were really boring, and unless the characters grab you right away, it doesn't matter how good the plot is. I'm sure you'd agree."

Mrs. Moto meowed loudly, then jumped onto my shoulders. I pulled her into my arms and snuggled her against my neck. "You'd be a great character in a book, wouldn't you? There wouldn't even have to be a plot. Just a bunch of scenes of you doing cute things. If you kept a journal of what you did every day, we could publish that. It'd be a bestseller."

The door burst open, startling Mrs. Moto and causing her to dig her claws into my chest. But when she saw who had entered the lounge, she meowed, then jumped onto the floor to greet her admirers.

"Here, kitty, kitty," Katy called. She sat on the floor and coaxed the cat into her lap. Her little brother, Sam, plopped down next to her, and they took turns petting Mrs. Moto. While the three of them were occupied, I sat back down on the couch and pulled a sewing kit out of my bag. I picked the cat costume up and started to stitch the zipper in place.

"Ouch!" I said as I pricked my finger with the needle.

"Are you okay?" Katy asked.

"I'll be fine." I walked over to the kitchenette, which ran along one side of the lounge, and grabbed a paper towel. Pressing down on my wound, I sat at the small table by the window and stared outside. There was nothing quite like people-watching at a marina. The types of folks who were drawn to living on boats were often quirky and had fascinating backstories. Some of them were trying to reinvent themselves, escaping from the day-to-day grind of working in a corporate job. Others were drawn to the sea and wanted to enjoy a simple life off the grid. And then there were those whose backstories remained a mystery, like Wanda. How had she ended up in Coconut Cove at the Palm Tree Marina?

"What's this?" Katy asked, pointing at Mrs. Moto's costume.

"Yeah, what's this?" Sam echoed as he put part of the costume on his head.

"It's for the pet-costume competition," I said.

"Cats don't wear costumes," Katy said. "Only dogs do."

"This cat does." I removed the piece from Sam's head and smoothed it out. "Don't you think she's going to look adorable in it?"

"What is it?" Sam asked.

"Don't you recognize it?" They both shook their heads. "We really need to do something about the educational system in our country."

"I don't like school," Sam said.

"You're only five," I said. "What's not to like about school? Aren't there crayons involved?"

Katy tugged on my arm. "I like school. My teacher puts stickers on my worksheets."

"Stickers are good," I said. "We could all use more stickers in our lives."

While the three of us were talking about our favorite stickers—Katy was partial to dinosaurs while Sam liked the ones from the latest Pixar movie—Ned came into the lounge. "There the two of you are," he said. "Your mom is here to pick you up. She's in a rush, so you better hurry up. Give your grandpa a kiss goodbye first though."

After both Ned and Mrs. Moto got kisses goodbye, he walked over to the coffee machine. "Want a cup, Mollie?"

"That would be great. Extra cream if you have it."

Ned brought two mugs over and set them on the coffee table. As he settled into the couch, the pile of books on the floor caught his eye. "What's that about?"

"Mrs. Moto was trying to pick something out to read. She likes a good bedtime story. Don't worry. I'll put everything back later." I took a sip of my coffee. It was delicious—pure caffeine and half-and-half. Not a rutabaga to be found. "Ben was telling us about Emily's memorial service earlier."

"It sounds like it will be a nice tribute to her," Ned said. "You guys are still coming, aren't you?"

"Of course...although now it might be a little weird."

"Weird?" After I explained the connection between Emily's father and Scooter's business dealings, Ned frowned. "That is strange. But I hope you'll still attend the service. Jeff doesn't have anything to do with Van der Byl's company, and the memorial is really about supporting Jeff during his time of grief."

"You're right. I'm sure Scooter will see

it that way." I went to the fridge and added some more cream to my cup to cool it down. As I stirred my coffee, I said, "Thinking about it, the memorial service might also be a good opportunity to talk to some of Emily's family and friends. Maybe they can shed some light on what this contract dispute is all about."

"She doesn't have any family, remember?"

I sat back down on the couch next to Mrs. Moto and scratched her belly. "That's right. But her friends will be there."

"I'm not sure about that either. According to Jeff, Emily led a pretty sheltered life. I don't think she had too many friends, and any that she had live on Destiny Key."

"So, why wouldn't they come? There's a ferry from the island to the mainland."

"You haven't lived here long enough to know much about Destiny Key. The inhabitants are a pretty reclusive bunch. They rarely leave the island."

"Makes you wonder how Jeff met Emily," I said.

Ned smiled. "Sometimes, I think you have more curiosity than a cat."

"Hopefully I have as many lives," I said.

"I think you must have, considering the dangerous situations you've found yourself in. How many bodies is it that you've found in Coconut Cove?"

I sighed. Tallying up my murder victim count seemed to be a popular pastime among local residents. I think they liked to keep their math skills sharp. "Five," I said. "But getting back to Jeff, you've got to be curious about how he met Emily too. We'll have to ask him about it at the memorial."

"That would probably be the perfect opportunity. He'll want to reminisce about his time with her. And it might also be your only opportunity, as he's leaving on a business trip next week."

"What kind of business is he in?" I asked.

"He's a pharmaceutical sales rep," Ned said. "He's got a lot of big clients all over the country. Internationally too."

I thought back to the disagreement that Jeff and Chief Dalton's ex-wife had had over herbal remedies versus drugs that doctors prescribed. Jeff had certainly seemed to know a lot about the subject and had warned us of the dangers of medicines that weren't regulated. If only we had known at the time that his warnings would turn out to be prescient. Emily did end up dying as a result of being poisoned by an overdose of an herbal remedy.

* * *

After Ned left, I picked the books up off the floor and set them back on the shelf. All except one—a cozy mystery that featured a corgi—which I decided to borrow. Although Mrs. Moto would have preferred a book that had a cat as a central character, I thought it would be fun to read about how a dog helped solve a murder investigation. Plus, it might give us some insight into the canine mind and get a leg up on the pet-costume competition.

Next, I washed the mugs in the sink and put them in the drying rack. After wiping down the counter, I tried to shoo Mrs. Moto off the table by the window so I could clean it as well. She wasn't having it. Instead, she pawed at a brown leather notebook, which was sitting next to a set of salt and pepper shakers and a napkin dispenser. She poked her nose in between the pages and pushed the front cover open.

"We have our own book," I said, showing her the corgi mystery. "Why don't you sleep on that instead of someone else's?" Mrs. Moto rolled on her back and stretched out all four of her legs, obscuring the pages. I lifted her off and set her on the chair. She hopped back on the table and made a beeline for the notebook. This time, I used more common sense. I pulled a napkin out of the dispenser, crumpled it up, and tossed it across the room. While she bounded after it, I picked the notebook up to close it. That's when I recognized the distinctive green ink, precise, compact letters, and dots over the *i*'s and *j*'s as Wanda's handiwork.

She must have forgotten it. Maybe it was a journal of some kind. I decided to stop by her boat to return it to her. But before I could get up to collect my bag and the pet costume, Mrs. Moto jumped back on the table and butted her head against my arm, jostling the book out of my hand. She used her nose again to push several of the pages over. Then she sat on top of the open notebook and yowled.

"What is going on with you?" I plucked the cat off and placed her in my lap. She continued to yowl. "I wish you'd use your words," I said. "Although, I guess you are. Your feline equivalent of words. What are you trying to say?"

Mrs. Moto reached out and pressed her paw on the notebook before staring intently at me. "Do you want me to read this? Don't you think that would be nosy, reading someone's journal?"

When it comes to stare-downs, my cat always wins. I finally relented and pulled the notebook toward me. It was a journal. The page that Mrs. Moto had opened the notebook to was dated a couple of weeks prior. I shivered as I read what Wanda had written:

I made a vow on my sister's grave that I would avenge her death. But I was a coward. I could never bring myself to do what needed to be done. To destroy the person who had destroyed my sister. Year after year went by and I did nothing. I just waited and watched. No action, no vengeance, just waiting and watching. An exile without any purpose.

I can't wait and watch anymore. Not with her flaunting it in my face. Her success, her happiness, her youth. All of that should have been my sister's. She doesn't deserve it. She doesn't deserve anything.

This time it's going to be different. This time I'm going to be strong. This time I'm going to do what needs to be done.

I felt my skin go clammy. I put the journal down on the table, then scooped Mrs. Moto up and hugged her, burrowing my face in her fur. She licked my cheek before wriggling out of my arms. She flipped a few more pages over with her paw and meowed quietly. I took a deep breath, then bent over the book. This entry was from Monday.

How could the wrong girl have been

taken? How could this have happened? How am I supposed to mourn while I'm in exile?

I can hear my sister from her grave, calling to me. Don't worry, dear sister, this time, she will die.

CHAPTER 13
THE WISDOM OF YODA

Holy buckets! What would you do if you had read something like that? Wanda seemed like such an ordinary woman—she lived on a sailboat, made money doing food demonstrations at the grocery store, wore legwarmers, and led a quiet life—but I guess she wasn't ordinary after all. Unless scribbling homicidal journal entries was normal. I'm pretty sure it wasn't.

One of my favorite quotes from *The Empire Strikes Back* popped into my head: "Once you start down the dark path, forever will it dominate your destiny." I had always liked how Yoda uttered that phrase with that cute speech pattern and accent of his, but now it had taken on a new meaning. Wanda's grief over her sister's death had caused her to take a very, very dark path toward murder. And not just one murder, but two murders. Penelope's life was in danger.

"Come on, Mrs. Moto," I said. "We've got to get out of here!"

I grabbed the journal and stuck it in my bag along with the corgi mystery and the pet costume. Mrs. Moto must have sensed the urgency of our mission, because she sat quietly while I put her harness and leash on.

We dashed out the door while I dialed the chief. "What do you mean he isn't at the police station?" I demanded of the woman who answered the phone. "He's at the festival? Doesn't he know there's a murderer on the loose?"

I hung up and quickly texted Penelope, warning her to avoid Wanda. Then I sped toward the waterfront park. After asking around, I heard that the chief was where I least expected him to be—at his ex-wife's art booth.

Anabel was busy with some potential customers, helping them to decide which painting would look better displayed over their mantel. My vote would have been for the one of fairies dancing around a toadstool, but they seemed partial to one of an elf family picnicking on a beach. The chief was sitting on a stool underneath a nearby tree feeding Frick and Frack treats.

"There you are!" I said after I caught my breath. "I've been searching for you everywhere!"

The burly man stood, then pointed at the doggie bed in the corner of Anabel's stand. "Lie down." After the Yorkies were convinced to settle down, he turned to me and raised both of his eyebrows. "Looks like you've found me."

I reached into my bag and thrust the evidence into his hands. "Read this."

"I'm not sure this is my cup of tea," the chief said. "Now, if it was about Yorkies instead of a corgi, then maybe."

"Oops. Sorry, wrong one," I said, exchanging the cozy mystery for the journal.

"It's nicely bound," he said, turning it over in his hands. "I like the decorative pattern on the leather."

"I'm not showing you this because of how it looks. It's proof that Wanda is the murderer." I grabbed the journal out of his hands, flipped the pages to the relevant entries, and passed it back to him. "Start here."

The chief's eyebrows were eerily still while he was reading. "Where did you find this?" he asked when he was finished.

"I didn't find it. Mrs. Moto did."

"Of course she did."

"Really, she did. It was sitting on the table in the marina lounge. I didn't pay any attention to it until Mrs. Moto pointed out its significance."

"I see. Will you excuse me for a moment?" The chief walked toward the waterfront while he talked to someone on his phone. I desperately wanted to follow him and listen in, but Anabel had finished up with her customers and wanted to know what was going on.

"I've just given your ex-husband an important clue that's going to crack open the murder investigation and save someone's life. He's probably on his way to arrest the culprit now."

She put her hands over her mouth and gasped. "I hope Tiny takes backup. I always get so worried." Frick and Frack, no doubt sensing their mom's distress, rushed over and began barking. She bent down and gave them a cuddle. "It's okay. Your daddy is going to be okay."

Mrs. Moto decided to get in on the cuddling. She barged in between the two dogs and butted Anabel's hand, catching her by surprise. I held my breath, waiting to see how she would react. "Okay, but just this once," Anabel said as she tentatively scratched the top of Mrs. Moto's head.

"Can I get you anything?" I asked. "You seem a little shaky."

"Can you grab me a rutabaga juice? Feel free to get one for yourself too."

"I think I'll pass," I said. "Why don't you go sit on that stool and I'll bring it over."

While I dug through the assortment of bottles in the cooler—who knew there were so many varieties of rutabaga juice available—Frick and Frack crawled into their doggie bed. Mrs. Moto followed, her leash dragging behind her. The three of them looked pretty adorable snuggled up together.

"I used to find her in my condo like that," Anabel said. "When she wasn't napping with Frick and Frack, I'd find her eating their dog food."

I sat on the ground next to Anabel and ran my fingers through the cool grass, trying to figure out how to broach the subject of the letter she had sent us. After a few moments, I went for the direct approach. "Listen, I'm really sorry she kept getting into your place, but why didn't you just talk to us about it and let us know it was a problem?"

"I don't know." She fiddled with the lid on her juice bottle while she stared at the people wandering through the booths, hunting for that perfect souvenir from the Coconut Cove Boating Festival. "I guess, if I'm honest, it's because it gave me an excuse to talk with Tiny. He came over one afternoon and listened to me complain about the cat hair. It was nice having a conversation with him about something other than joint custody of our dogs. I went to the station the next day to talk with him about it some more, and he told me he didn't have time. Then I think things just escalated from there. I guess I took out my anger at Tiny on you guys."

"I get it," I said. "Scooter tells me that sometimes I let things get out of hand."

"Do you think we could just forget about everything that's happened and move on?"

"Sure," I said. "Water under the bridge." Mrs. Moto looked at us and meowed softly. "I think she forgives you too. Either that or she wants one of those dog treats."

* * *

I had another sleepless night. If Chief Dalton thought I had an overactive imagination during my waking hours, he'd be amazed at what my mind came up with while I was sleeping. My nightmares were getting stranger and stranger. The latest one featured giant rutabagas wearing Trixie Tremblay T-shirts and polka-dotted legwarmers and chasing after me on stilts. I wasn't sure what I found more disturbing—the fact that the rutabagas had somehow grown legs and could move around unaided or the fact that I thought their legwarmers were cute.

While Scooter made our morning smoothies, I checked my phone. Despite having sent Penelope several texts warning her about Wanda the previous day, she hadn't replied. My stomach churned. I really hoped that meant that Wanda hadn't gotten to her first. I dialed the police station and asked to be connected to the chief. After the receptionist asked who was calling, she told me that the chief had left a message for me: "No comment."

I choked down my smoothie while drawing some unflattering pictures of the chief's eyebrows in my notebook. It was a therapeutic way to deal with my annoyance. They actually looked very realistic. Maybe I was more artistic than I realized. I'd have to show my drawings to Anabel and ask her what she thought. Art classes might be in my future.

I finally dragged myself out of bed and headed to the waterfront park. I was scheduled to man the FAROUT booth that morning. If I hadn't been running late, I would have stopped by the Sugar Shack to check on Penelope beforehand. Fortunately, I didn't have plans for the afternoon, which would give me time to visit her, as well as finish Mrs. Moto's costume.

Anabel was setting up her artwork when I got there. I helped her hang a large painting of a leprechaun riding on the back of the Loch Ness monster while it swam through the water. I have to confess that I was a little confused by it at first—leprechauns were indigenous to Ireland and the Loch Ness monster lived in Scotland—but then she explained that the Loch Ness monster had actually spread worldwide. There was even one living in Lake Okeechobee in the middle of Florida. It was quite reclusive, so most people weren't aware that it was there.

Then she confided to me that if she sold that painting, it would cover her mortgage payments for several months. After hearing that, I definitely decided to look into art classes. Perhaps I could make a small fortune selling watercolor paintings of the chief's eyebrows.

When I asked Anabel if she had heard from her ex-husband, she got a little teary-eyed, so I dropped the subject. I tried to reassure myself that he had everything under control. Surely, Wanda was locked up in a cell. Penelope's cell phone battery had died, and she was safe and sound at the Sugar Shack whipping up a batch of muffins. At least, that's what I told myself.

I was organizing T-shirts when I heard a cheery voice call out, "Get your free Rutamentals sample here!" My jaw dropped when I saw Wanda standing only a few feet away holding a large tray and trying to convince people about the health benefits of carob-covered rutabagas. My hands started shaking, and the T-shirts tumbled to the ground. As I bent down to pick them up, I bumped my head against the table. When I looked up, I found myself staring into a pair of homicidal green eyes.

"What are you doing here?" I spluttered. I reached into my bag and tried to pull out something to protect myself with. The best I could come up with was my trusty roll of breath mints. If only I had stuck with those karate classes. Fresh breath wasn't really going to be an effective self-defense strategy. Bad breath maybe, but not fresh, minty breath.

"One of the other gals is watching the

Rutamentals booth, so I decided to stroll through the park and hand out samples." She waved a gooey brown lump in front of my face. "One taste of these and people will be flocking to our booth to sign up for the program. Go on, try it. You'll be surprised how much carob tastes like chocolate."

I took a step backward. "Surprised? I'll tell you what I'm surprised about, that you're walking around free."

Wanda set the tray on the table and wagged her finger at me. "You know, I should be mad at you. That was very naughty what you did—giving the chief my journal. It was private."

I glanced over at Anabel and frantically tried to make eye contact. Fortunately for her, she was busy making a sale. Unfortunately for me, she didn't notice I was alone with a homicidal maniac.

"Cat got your tongue?" Wanda asked. "Speaking of, where is that cat of yours?

Chief Dalton said she found my journal."

For once I was glad Mrs. Moto had decided to stay on the boat with Scooter rather than keep me company. "Don't you dare hurt her!"

Wanda pursed her lips. "Why would I hurt her? Don't you think you're overreacting?" She smiled. "Kind of like how you overreacted when you read my journal. Like I told the chief, it didn't mean anything. It's just an exercise my therapist has me do. By writing about things that anger or frustrate us on a daily basis, we can process our feelings and let go of our negative emotions."

"The things you wrote about were pretty out there. These weren't everyday frustrations you were talking about," I said. "You wrote about murder, for goodness' sake."

"You're right, Mollie. I wrote about some serious things." She sighed. "I've experienced some very painful things in my past. I'm still angry to this day about what happened to my sister. But you have to believe me. I would never actually hurt anyone."

"What exactly happened to your sister?"

Her eyes welled up with tears. "My therapist says I should confide in other people. I've never told anyone other than him what happened, but since you've read my journal, I might as well tell you." She pointed at the chairs set up behind the table. "Mind if I sit down?"

"Uh, sure," I said. There were enough people milling around that I didn't think she'd try anything. Still, to be on the safe side, I didn't plan on eating anything that she had prepared. Not even poison could enhance the taste of rutabaga.

Wanda ran her fingers through her long dark hair and took a deep breath. "Okay, here goes. My brother-in-law killed my sister."

"That's awful! He murdered her?"

"She committed suicide, but he drove her to it. Although it wasn't murder in the technical sense, she wouldn't be dead if it wasn't for him. He betrayed her in the worst possible way." Tears flowed down her cheeks. "She was only twenty-five. She left behind a..." I handed her a tissue. After blowing her nose, she continued. "She left behind a beautiful four-year-old girl. I couldn't bear it. My sister and I had been so close. We did everything together. We were best friends."

Wanda started sobbing uncontrollably. I shifted uneasily in my chair. People were staring at us. Anabel mouthed, "Are you okay?"

I nodded, then gently patted the distraught woman on her back. "There, there," I said, which was such a stupid thing to say. What do people mean when they say that while consoling someone? It's not like you're pointing at something when you say it—There,

there, look at that there. Over there. There, there. *Get a grip, Mollie,* I told myself. *You're starting to channel Dr. Seuss.*

"Can I get you something to drink?" I asked. Another pretty banal thing to say, but it got Dr. Seuss out of my head.

"Do you have any rutabaga juice?" she asked.

"You're sure you don't want something with some sugar and caffeine instead? That's what I turn to when I'm stressed."

Wanda glanced down at her Trixie Tremblay T-shirt. "No, I'll stick with the juice. Live Healthy, Live Long, Live Strong."

"Okay, coming right up." I scooted over to Anabel's booth. "Can I snag a juice from you?"

"Sure." She scratched her head. "Didn't you tell me that she's a murderer?"

"Uh-huh."

"Um, far be it from me to judge, but do

you think it's a good idea to be having a drink with her?"

I held up my hands. "Honestly, I don't know what to think right now. When I read her journal yesterday, I was convinced she was a killer. But now, I'm not so sure. She said her therapist told her to write that stuff down. You wouldn't believe the horrifying story she told me about her sister. I think she might just be a messed-up lady."

"Hmm. Maybe you're right. Besides, if she was a killer, Tiny would have locked her up."

A sense of relief washed over me. "That's true. She isn't in custody, so her story must have checked out." I squeezed Anabel's hand. "Thanks for that and for the juice."

After I handed Wanda the bottle, I apologized for reading her journal and giving it to the police.

"That's okay. I probably would have done the same thing in your shoes," she said. While she sipped her juice, I noticed a slight grimace on her face. Was it possible that the Trixie Tremblay spokesperson didn't like the taste of the products she was selling? "You sure you don't want some?" Wanda asked.

"Oh, I'm sure. I think I'll stick to water." I tapped my finger on my lips. "I hope you don't mind me asking, but who were you talking about in your journal? Were the women you wrote about Emily and Penelope?"

Wanda's eyes grew wide, and she started coughing. She set her bottle on the table. "Sorry, it must have gone down the wrong way. Why would I have written about Emily and Penelope? I didn't really know either of them."

"But you wrote about the wrong girl dying. I assumed that referred to Emily. Then you talked about another girl who didn't deserve to live. Wasn't that a reference to Penelope?"

"Goodness, no. It doesn't have

anything to do with present-day. I was writing about what happened in the past. The wrong girl was my sister. She didn't deserve to die."

"Then who was the other girl?"

Wanda bit her lip. "My brother-in-law had an affair. It referred to his mistress. It's what drove my sister to…"

I squeezed her hands. "It's okay. I didn't mean to dig up painful memories."

She pulled her hands back and folded them in her lap. "The chief did say that you fancy yourself an amateur investigator. If you're really interested in who's after Penelope, then you might want to talk to Alan."

"Alan?" I asked in disbelief. "Why would he want to kill her?"

"He was in love with Penelope, but she refused to go out with him. He got really angry."

"Angry enough to kill?"

"Emily's death is proof of that," she said.

I thought about this for a minute. If you had asked me a few weeks ago if mild-mannered, meek-as-a-mouse Alan could fly into a jealous rage and murder someone, I would have laughed. But I remembered the confrontation he'd had with Jeff before the sailing race. There had been a look in Alan's eyes that had frightened me. Maybe he was capable of violence.

Wanda patted my hand. "The chief and I had a long talk about it. You don't need to worry. He has everything under control. They're conducting some lab tests. Once he gets the results back, he'll arrest Alan, and Coconut Cove can go back to being the pleasant, sleepy tourist town that it is."

* * *

"Are you ready to go, my little Milk Dud?" Scooter asked.

"Well, that depends on where we're

going," I said. "Is there going to be lunch involved?"

"I think that could be arranged."

"Then I'll be ready in five minutes." After I explained to the volunteer who had arrived at the FAROUT booth for the afternoon shift which T-shirts were on sale, I grabbed my bag and put my arm through Scooter's. "Where do you want to eat at?"

"I would say the Rutamentals booth, but after you told me about Wanda's journal, I'm hesitant to go there."

I was torn. Scooter was on the cusp of being persuaded to have hot dogs instead of rutabagas. If I let him continue to believe that Wanda had a deft touch with using poison as a seasoning, that would be unfair to her. But the price of telling him about her therapy and her tragic past was that he'd probably opt for the "healthy" choice.

My big mistake was glancing up at

him. One look at those dark-brown puppy-dog eyes of his and I sang like a canary. I waited nervously while he thought about what I had said. For the record, it turned out that telling the truth worked in my favor this time.

"Hmm. I suppose that means we could eat something that has Trixie Tremblay's blessing on it," Scooter said. "But maybe we deserve a treat. We've been doing really well on our diet. I'm sure having one hot dog wouldn't do any harm."

Falling off the wagon never tasted so good, I thought to myself as I piled extra sauerkraut on my dog. Scooter moaned with pleasure as he took a bite of his. After handing him an extra napkin, I went in for the kill. "Wanna get some ice cream after this?"

Scooter took a swallow of his soda. "I'm not sure we should."

"We don't have to get sundaes," I said. "They sell small cones. Surely, one little scoop of ice cream would be okay. Even Trixie Tremblay must have a treat from time to time."

"I guess…"

"Good. I'm glad we're in agreement." I wiped some mustard off Scooter's cheek. "You won't regret this."

After we got our dessert—double chocolate chip for me and raspberry swirl for Scooter—we walked toward the waterfront and sat at one of the picnic tables next to the public docks. Fishing and charter boats tied up there to offload their catch and pick up passengers. One of Norm's boats, the newly christened *ET*, was coming into port. A bunch of college-aged kids on spring break disembarked. A good-natured argument broke out about who had caught the biggest fish.

"It seems like Norm's charter business is benefiting from visitors to the festival," I said.

Scooter licked the ice cream that was

dripping down the side of his cone. "Do you think he'll be able to juggle his business with being mayor?"

"Bite your tongue," I said. "Let's pray he doesn't get elected."

"Isn't that Mike over there?" Scooter smiled. "Hopefully, he's not making a campaign contribution."

"Maybe it's time that you got into politics," I mused. "I think you'd make a fine mayor. You tick all the boxes— you're honest, trustworthy, reliable, and you look good in green."

"What does green have to do with running for office?"

"Isn't it obvious? Green has—"

"Hey there," Mike said. He slapped Scooter on his back, jostling his elbow. I looked on in dismay as his ice cream toppled off his cone and onto the table. "Oh, man, I'm sorry about that. Let me get you another one."

"No, it's okay," Scooter said glumly. "It was probably a sign that I shouldn't be eating it."

I hurriedly finished my ice cream before he decided that the sign also applied to me. "What were you doing talking to Norm?" I asked as I licked the last of the double chocolate chip off my fingers. "I'm surprised to see the two of you so chummy after the sailboat accident."

Mike stroked his goatee. "We came to an agreement."

"You mean he paid you off?" I asked.

"Something like that. Let's just say we've put our differences aside for the moment to focus on something more important—making the arrangements for Emily's memorial service tomorrow. Jeff asked if I could help out."

"He chartered Norm's boat?" Scooter asked.

"Yeah. He gave him a good rate."

"Norm must want something from him," I said.

Scooter laughed. "His vote." He turned

to Mike. "It's nice of you to help Jeff out."

"That's what friends are for," he said. "And I have an idea of what she would have wanted. Plenty of yellow roses and the soundtrack to *Mamma Mia!*"

"I thought you didn't know Emily," I said. "How would you know about the flowers and music?"

"It's hot today, isn't it," Mike said. He grabbed one of the napkins on the table and wiped his brow.

"Not really," I said. "It's actually quite pleasant. I don't think the temperature is why you're breaking out in a sweat." I patted the seat next to me. "Why don't you take a load off."

"Um, I should probably get going," Mike said with a slight stammer.

"Sit," I said, doing my best imitation of Nancy. It worked. Mike planted his butt on the bench next to me. "What I don't understand is why you've been pretending not to know Emily. I already know you drew up her will."

Mike's jaw dropped. "You do?"

"I do now." By this point, his napkin was soaking wet. I passed him another. "Why have you been keeping it a secret? Wouldn't it impress potential clients if they knew you were doing work for such a big estate?"

"It wasn't my idea," he said. "Her family is very secretive. They don't like outsiders knowing about their business. When I first started working for her father—"

"Maarten van der Byl, right?" Scooter asked.

Mike nodded slowly, then leaned forward. "You might want to keep that name to yourself," he said softly.

Scooter banged his fist on the table. "Why should I do that? He's putting the screws into me from the grave. Don't pretend like you didn't know it was his company that I've been having contract disputes with."

Stunned by my husband's uncharacteristic outburst, I found myself at a loss as to what to say next. I watched as Scooter drummed his fingers on the table while Mike tried his best to avoid eye contact. "How about some more ice cream?" I suggested. Unsurprisingly, that fell flat.

"How about some answers, Mike," Scooter said.

"The Van der Byls are one of the families who founded Destiny Key. They have a lot of money, and they use that to buy people's silence." He gulped. "Including mine. I've done some things I'm not proud of."

"Like trying to destroy my company."

"No," Mike said. "I didn't have anything to do with Mr. Van der Byl's business interests. The only thing I dealt with was the family's estate planning."

"Then you can tell us about Emily's will," I said.

Mike blanched. "No. I can't."

"You're going to tell us something," Scooter said.

"Listen, I know the firm that represents the Van der Byl's business side of things. Maybe I can try to find out what's going on with the contract."

"And you can tell us about Emily," I said.

"I've already told everything I know to the police," Mike said.

I furrowed my brow. "Does that mean you're a suspect?" At the rate sweat was dripping down his face, Mike was in danger of becoming dehydrated. I offered him some of my water.

"Me? Why would I be a suspect? I don't stand to gain anything from Emily's death. But if you want to know who I think the police have in their sights, I can—"

Before Mike could spill the beans, he was interrupted by the screams of a young girl. She had her hands over her mouth and was staring at something lying on the ground next to the dock.

The three of us leaped up and raced toward her. It turned out it wasn't a something lying on the ground. It was a someone, and her name was Wanda.

I leaned down to check on her while Scooter dialed 911. She was breathing shallowly, her eyelids fluttering as she fought to stay conscious. As I stroked her forehead and told her that help was on the way, she whispered my name.

"Ssh. Don't say anything. Save your breath, Wanda," I said.

"Mollie," she said weakly. I put my ear against her mouth to hear her better. "Alan. It was Alan. He poisoned me."

CHAPTER 14
MICE IN TUTUS

The Coconut Cove grapevine was working overtime. I woke up to several texts updating me on Wanda's status. She was going to be fine, but the doctor wanted to keep her in the hospital for another day for observation. With any luck, she'd be discharged on Saturday morning.

The grapevine was silent on two key issues: (1) what Wanda had been poisoned with and (2) what the story with Alan was. I didn't even bother calling the police station for an update, as I was sure I'd get a two-word response: "No comment." So I fired up my laptop to do my own research.

After being distracted for a few minutes by cat videos on YouTube (could Mrs. Moto be the next internet sensation?), I typed Alan's name into the search bar, pressed Enter, and held my breath. Fortunately, Google searches took less than a second to pull up a list of results, so I didn't really have to hold my breath, something I was never very good at. I always ended up hiccoughing, which wasn't great when you were trying to rescue the sunglasses your cat had batted into the deep end of the pool.

While Alan didn't make a huge impression in real life, preferring to blend into the background, he had a big presence online. I found three websites —one for his photography business, one for his nonfiction books (apparently his DIY guide on how to winterize composting toilets hit the bestseller list in Mongolia), and a blog where he posted articles on a number of fascinating topics, including…wait for it…yep, you guessed it—poisonous substances.

Our mild-mannered photographer wasn't as mild-mannered as he seemed. His descriptions of what different poisons could do to the human body were pretty gruesome. I was particularly interested in his series of posts on the use of poisons in different television shows. He rated each one on how difficult it was for the murderer to obtain the poison in question and how realistic the depiction of the poisoning was. In his introduction, he stated that he wanted to provide this information as a resource for mystery writers. Then he added a disclaimer: "Don't try any of these at home, unless you can be sure you won't get caught. LOL!"

LOL indeed. It was time to find out more about Alan's background. I clicked on his bio. Turns out he had an advanced degree in biology and had worked in a research lab for many years. After becoming a little too attached to the test mice (he kept sneaking them into his briefcase and taking them home), he had an epiphany —by "epiphany," I think he meant he had been fired for mice-napping—and he made a career change, becoming a photographer.

Alan also had a YouTube channel, which featured a number of videos of mice doing adorable things. Mrs. Moto was entranced by the tiny outfits they wore while they walked across a miniature balance beam. I was entranced by the beadwork on their tutus. Alan apparently was handy not just with winterizing composting toilets but also with needlework.

As I watched a mouse swinging on a

trapeze, I realized that Alan had never shown me the video he had taken the day of the cake competition. Was that because it revealed him doing something suspicious like poisoning Penelope's slice of cake? Nah, that couldn't be it. If that had been captured on video, the chief would have arrested him for the murder at the outset. Still, I wondered if there was something the police had missed that Alan didn't want me to see.

I checked my phone again. Still no helpful messages about what was going on with Wanda and Alan. It was time to go directly to the ultimate source of information in Coconut Cove—the Sailor's Corner Cafe.

* * *

"*Hola.* What can I get you, *chica*?" Alejandra asked as she set a cup of coffee down in front of me.

"Nothing, just the coffee," I said in an admirable display of willpower.

"Are you sure? The chef's got a new special—smothered fries."

"What are they smothered in?" I asked. "Not that I want any. It's just professional curiosity."

"Gravy, cheese, bacon, onions, bell peppers, sour cream, grated rutabaga —"

"Did you say rutabaga?"

"It's the latest craze," she said. "People are requesting it on everything. Even if they're not hardcore into Rutamentals, they're adding small amounts of rutabaga to other dishes to get the health benefits. So, one order of fries for you?"

I shuddered. "Thanks, but I think I'll stick to coffee."

A few minutes later, I was chowing down on smothered fries, minus the rutabaga. Willpower is so overrated.

When Alejandra came back to refill my

coffee, I asked her if she had overheard any juicy tidbits during the morning rush. She looked around the cafe. The few people who were there had been served, and no one was waiting to be seated. She slid into the chair opposite me and rolled her shoulders back and forth. "I'm so stiff," she said.

"Waitressing is hard work," I said.

"Nah, that's a piece of cake compared to the Trixie Tremblay boot camp I enrolled in." She twisted her head from side to side, then stretched her arms over her head.

"Don't tell me you're a convert too."

"I sure am, *chica*. I have so much more energy now. You should try it."

I glanced under the table. Sure enough, Alejandra was wearing legwarmers. How had I missed them earlier? Please tell me that Scooter hadn't begun sporting legwarmers, and I had failed to notice.

"I get enough exercise working on our

boat," I said.

"Fair enough, but remember how you were asking me if I'd heard any good gossip about the poisonings?" I nodded. "Well, the place to hear what's really going on isn't here at the cafe, it's at the boot camp. You won't believe what I heard this morning."

I leaned forward, eager for her to spill the beans. She glanced around to make sure that no one needed anything. "Penelope told me that—"

"Wait a minute. This is huge news!"

"But I haven't told you any news yet."

"Yes, you have. You said Penelope was at the Trixie Tremblay boot camp. Do you know what that means?" Alejandra shook her head. "It means the end of the Sugar Shack as we know it. She's going to stop serving cookies, pies, cakes, basically everything that makes life worth living."

"Relax. It was the first time Penelope had attended. A friend invited her. She's been going a bit stir crazy—the police have tried to limit her movements to the bakery and her home, and she has protection around the clock. But she was able to convince them to let her attend an exercise class, provided one of the officers went with her."

"So she's not wearing legwarmers yet?"

Alejandra smiled. "Nope, I think you're safe for now. Although she was talking about creating a special line of Trixie Tremblay–inspired muffins."

"That's a relief. So what was your news?"

"Between you and me, Penelope told me about Alan asking her out."

"Ooh, that's interesting. Wanda mentioned something about that." I used a spoon to scoop up the last of the gravy from my plate. "What happened?"

"He came to the Sugar Shack to do an interview with her. At first, the questions seemed pretty normal. He asked how she got into baking, about the culinary awards she had won, the challenges in starting your own business, that kind of thing. Then he began asking her some really odd questions. Originally, she thought the interview was for the local newspaper, but when the article never got published, she checked and found out he had made that up."

"What kinds of questions did he ask?"

"About her family. He had some information on her mother, but he asked her what she knew regarding her father." Alejandra did a few more stretches. "The thing is, she doesn't know anything about her father. Her mom raised her on her own, and she clammed up whenever Penelope would ask her about her father. Alan's questions made her feel really uncomfortable."

"I hope she told him that he was asking inappropriate things."

"You know what she's like. She's so

sweet. She never tells anyone when she doesn't like something. She can't stand hurting people's feelings."

I remembered how Penelope hadn't wanted to award prizes at the cake competition. I didn't recall her saying anything negative about anyone's cake. Nancy could probably learn a thing or two from her about diplomacy. "So what happened next?" I asked.

"He switched over to the topic of genetic diseases. He asked her if she had any medical conditions."

"Surely she slugged him by this point."

"Nope. She kept smiling and offering him cookies."

"She's too sweet for her own good," I said.

"Good thing she owns a bakery. A sweet lady selling sweet things. It's the perfect fit for her." Alejandra did a few more neck stretches, then reluctantly got up from the table. "The lunchtime crowd is going to start coming in soon, and those tables aren't going to clean themselves."

As I finished sipping my coffee, I thought about Alan's devious behavior. Faking a newspaper interview to try to pry information out of Penelope was pretty low. Why in the world was he so interested in her family and her medical history?

While I pondered this, I sent my mom a text.

Any genetic diseases in our family I should know about?

I had come to the conclusion that I didn't have a secret twin sister named Mary. It had probably been my mom's idea of a joke. She rolled on the floor in laughter over knock-knock jokes, which gives you an idea of the sophistication of her humor. I was ninety-nine percent sure there was no way she'd forget to tell me that I had a sibling. But she might have forgotten to tell me something important about my medical history.

A few minutes later, she replied.

Do you mean like Mary' s large ears?

Great. We were back to this whole Mary business. I reached up and felt my ears. Were they misshapen too, like Jeff's and Mary's?

* * *

I ran into Alan at the place I least expected—the hairdresser's. I'm one of those people who puts off getting their hair cut until it's so out of control that even Mrs. Moto encourages me to wear a hat in public. Each time I visit the salon, I have renewed hope that it will be the time my frizzy hair is finally tamed once and for all. Instead, I squeal with delight at how sleek and shiny the stylist makes my hair, eagerly buy the latest miracle product, and step outside with a huge grin, only to find the unruly frizz resurfaces within ten minutes' time in the humidity.

Alan was in the back having his hair shampooed. I sat in the chair next to him while I waited for the hairdresser to get an industrial-size container of deep conditioner from the back. I was already convinced that the "Frizz Banishment Gel, Now with Extra Moisturizing Pearls of Liquid Gold and Imported from Siberia for Discerning Ladies" was going to be the answer to my dreams. Intellectually, I knew that it didn't contain any gold and that Siberia probably wasn't where you wanted your beauty products imported from. But I was happy to suspend disbelief. After all, I was certainly a discerning lady.

"Mollie, what are you doing here?" Alan whispered as a towel was wrapped around his head.

I pointed at my frizzy mane. "Turning this into a work of beauty. What about you?"

"I wanted to make an effort for Emily's

memorial service," he said.

"Exactly how long did you two date?" I asked.

"Long enough."

"And how long is that?"

"A week," he said as he fiddled with his smock. "But it was enough to know we were meant to be together. If only Jeff hadn't gotten in the way."

Before I could hear more about his ill-fated love affair with Emily, his hairdresser whisked him away to one of the stations. For the next ten minutes, I oohed and aahed during my shampoo. My body felt like it was melting into a puddle of happiness as my head was massaged with the Siberian miracle mix.

As luck would have it, I was shown to the station right next to Alan. I picked up where we left off. "I heard you asked Penelope out. Was that before or after you dated Emily?"

Alan spun his head toward me, causing his stylist to narrowly avoid nicking his ear with the scissors. "Where did you hear that?"

"Oh, you know how small towns are. Nothing stays secret for very long." Alan's hairdresser gently turned his head back toward the mirror and started snipping the hair on his neck. "You know what else isn't a secret," I added. "The fact that Wanda accused you of poisoning her."

Both of our stylists gasped. They were torn between wanting to keep a distance from a potential murderer and wanting to hear all the juicy tidbits so they could pass them on to their other clients. I did notice that Alan's hairdresser kept a firm grip on her scissors.

"That's not true," Alan said emphatically, staring at my reflection in the mirror. "I wasn't even at the festival yesterday. I was photographing a wedding seventy-five miles away from here."

"Can you prove that?" I asked.

He clenched his hands in his lap. "I've already been through this with the chief. There are plenty of witnesses, starting from the bride and groom down to the flower girl and ring bearer. Do you want to talk to them too?"

By this point, Alan's hairdresser had given up all pretense of cutting his hair. He set down his brush and scissors, sat in the chair next to Alan's, and eagerly listened to our exchange. Mine was still combing and sectioning my hair but in a very halfhearted way.

"Why do you think she tried to pin the blame on you? And more importantly, if you didn't do it, who did?"

"Wanda is vindictive," he said. "She doesn't understand what's involved in investigative journalism. She claimed I was sticking my nose in where it didn't belong, and she's been out to get me ever since."

"Well, were you?"

"Was I what?"

"Asking nosy questions?"

"It seems like you're the one asking nosy questions," Alan said with a surprisingly firm tone. It stunned me into silence for a few moments.

"You know, Alan, maybe we're going about this all wrong. You're not just a wedding photographer. You're also an investigative reporter and photojournalist, right?"

"That's correct. I'm in discussions with the local newspaper about a permanent role with them."

I had a feeling his dialogue with the newspaper might be a little one-sided, but I plowed on. "Well, I'm an investigative reporter for FAROUT. We should join forces. Between the two of us, we'd get to the bottom of what's going on a lot faster. You did help me out with my last case, after all."

He grinned from ear to ear. "That's a great idea! We'll be a detective team, like Nick and Nora from the *Thin Man* movies."

"No, they had a dog, Asta, and I'm a cat person."

"Sherlock Holmes and Dr. Watson?"

I shook my head. "I look funny in hats."

"The Hardy Boys?"

"Nope. Nancy Drew all the way for me," I said.

One of the stylists chimed in. "How about the guys from *CHiPs*? They had good hair."

Alan frowned. "That won't work. My mom won't let me ride a motorcycle."

"I've got it," I said. "Shawn Spencer and Burton Guster from *Psych*. You're Gus and I'm Shawn. Shawn pretends to be a psychic in the show. I've met a lot of psychics in my time, so I can pull that off."

"What does Gus do?"

"He has a really good sense of smell," I said. "You can smell things, right?"

Alan furrowed his brow. "Sure."

"What's your favorite scent?"

"I have a candle that smells like cotton candy. I also have a peanut butter scented one. It's—"

"Perfect. Burton Guster it is. Okay, now that that's settled, let's get down to business." I reached down, picked my bag off the floor, and whipped out my notebook. "Here's what I need to know…"

While the stylists worked on our hair, I managed to get Alan to tell me why he had asked Penelope all those strange questions about her family and genetic conditions. It turned out that Emily had put him up to it. On their first date—Alan took her to the video arcade—she suggested that he do a series of profiles on some of Coconut Cove's residents. He was excited about the idea and thought he could pitch it to the local newspaper. Before he could draw up a list of prominent citizens to interview, she handed him her own list. It had only three names on it: Wanda, Penelope, and one of Penelope's mother's old friends.

Penelope's name made some sense. She was a young, local, award-winning business owner, but the other two names didn't. Wanda led a relatively quiet life. She wasn't involved in community activities or the town council and didn't own a business. And speaking with an old friend of Penelope's mom and asking questions about her was just plain odd. Sure, Penelope's mom had worked at the library up until her death—and everyone loved library people—but even that, from Alan's point of view, didn't merit a profile in the paper.

Emily had given him a very specific set of questions to ask. While he rattled them off, I jotted down the highlights in my notebook:

Wanda

1 – When did she move from Destiny

Key to Coconut Cove?

At first Wanda denied being from Destiny Key, but after Alan showed her a copy of old property records, she said that she moved to Coconut Cove following the death of her sister twenty-five years ago.

2 – Does she have any family back on Destiny Key?

She stated that she was the only one left in her family. When pressed on the issue, she clammed up.

3 – Why did she leave Destiny Key?

At this point in the interview, she burst into tears. Alan felt terrible. He offered to take publicity shots of her Rutamentals food demonstrations for free to make it up to her.

<u>Penelope</u>

1 – What does she know about her family history? Where did her father come from?

She said she didn't know her father. He had died before she was born. Her mother didn't like to talk about him. Her mom became moody whenever Penelope asked questions about him, so she learned to stop bringing it up. She changed the subject and brought Alan a selection of pastries to try. His favorite was the chocolate éclair.

2 – Does she have any genetic conditions that she inherited from her parents?

Penelope was surprised by Alan's question, but after a while she told him about having a congenital heart condition. She was able to manage it with medications, but had to be careful with certain activities. She didn't know which side of the family she inherited it from. At this point in the interview, Penelope made Alan a latte.

3 – What's the secret to her puff pastry?

Penelope wouldn't share her secret recipe no matter how many times Alan asked.

Cindy, Penelope's Mom's Friend

1 – What was the family history of Penelope's mom? Where did she grow up?

Cindy didn't know anything about her background. They had children the same age. Cindy divorced when her daughter was quite young, so the two of them bonded as fellow single moms. But despite doing so much together, Cindy never learned anything about her life prior to Coconut Cove.

2 – When did she move to Coconut Cove?

A few months before Penelope was born.

3 – How did she support herself with a young baby?

She seemed to be financially independent. She wasn't rich, but she didn't have to worry about putting food on the table and was able to stay home with Penelope when she was young.

Later, she got a job working at the local library, but that seemed like it was more for something to do while her daughter was in school, not because she needed the money.

I asked Alan if by any chance Emily had broken up with him after he'd finished the interviews. He admitted that was the case, but was still convinced Jeff was the reason why Emily had ended things.

Eventually, we had to halt our conversation so that my hair could be blown out. It looked amazing! I asked Alan to take a picture of me so I could remember what I looked like before the humidity destroyed my sleek coiffure. As he showed me the photo, I remembered the video from the cake competition. In the spirit of our newfound partnership, he was more than happy to pull it up on my tablet.

"But you can't really tell what happened," I complained. "All I see is a bunch of people milling around. What we need is a clear shot of who put the poison on the cake slice."

Alan replayed the video at a slower speed. We watched as Nancy cut four slices from each cake—one for each judge—and placed them on the different-colored plates that Norm handed her. Penelope and Chief Dalton then carried the plates over to the small tables set up at the back for the judges. All the blue ones were placed on the chief's table, the green ones on Norm's table, the white ones on Nancy's table, and the ill-fated purple ones on Penelope's table.

"Okay, so it didn't happen then," I said. "You can clearly see Nancy's and Norm's hands as they plated up the cake slices. Neither of them got out a bottle and doused one of the slices with gelsemium. And it couldn't have been when Penelope and the chief carried the plates over. There's no way Penelope would poison herself, and if Chief Dalton did it, then we've got bigger things to worry about."

"Have a look here," Alan said. "After they set the cake slices on the tables, all the contestants and judges gathered around to check out the display."

"What's Scooter doing there?" I watched as he walked over to Penelope's table and looked from side to side for a few moments. "I thought Nancy forbade the general public from that side of the barrier."

"Look there," Alan said as he pointed at the screen. Scooter bent down and picked up a ball from the floor, then walked out of the frame. "I think he was retrieving it for those kids."

"And isn't that you?" I asked, pointing at a short man wearing a gray shirt.

"Uh-huh," he said. "I had my camera on a tripod at that point."

I watched as Alan stood with his back to the camera right in front of

Penelope's table all by himself. My earlier doubts about the newly christened "Burton Guster" resurfaced. Maybe he'd had an alibi for when Wanda was poisoned, but he could have still been responsible for what had happened to Emily.

"Hey, you don't think I did it, do you?" He fast-forwarded and then froze the picture. "See, that's you all by yourself by the cake. It could have been you too. In fact, it could have been any of us."

As we watched the rest of the video, my heart sank. He was right. Everyone had been by themselves in front of Penelope's table at one point or the other, and with the angle of the camera, there was no way of knowing if they had taken that opportunity to poison the cake.

"Ugh. We're no closer to finding out who did it." I tapped my fingers on the armrests of my chair. "Hey, wait a minute. What if someone came in the back door?"

"Easy enough to find out," Alan said. He tapped on my tablet for a few minutes, then passed it to me. "Here you go. The security footage from the camera in the courtyard."

"How did you get this?"

Alan shrugged. "Don't ask."

My estimation of him shot up. A man with hacking skills. That could come in handy in the future. It never pays to underestimate mild-mannered people. They often surprise you.

"So what does it show?" Alan asked.

"Only two people entered through the back—Emily and Mrs. Moto. I guess we're back to the drawing board."

Alan ran his fingers through his hair, studying his reflection in the mirror. "Mollie, can I ask you a serious question?"

"Sure."

"Do you think I should color my hair? Maybe go for dark brown like Scooter?

Women like tall, dark, and handsome men, don't they?"

"Um...it's what's on the inside that counts, not the outside," I said diplomatically.

Alan picked at his fingernails. "If that's the case, why did Emily break up with me?"

I didn't have the heart to tell him that it might have had something to do with his taste in scented candles or the fact that he had a YouTube channel featuring mice in tiny costumes. But I am convinced that there's someone out there for everyone. Once we nabbed the murderer, I planned to turn my attention to finding Alan the perfect woman. Provided, of course, that he didn't turn out to be the murderer himself. My skills at fixing people up on blind dates only went so far.

CHAPTER 15
WRINKLE-FREE CLOTHES

Once I got back from the hair salon, it was time to get ready for Emily's memorial service. I wasn't sure what to wear. Normally, I'd select a black dress and heels, but the service was being held on a boat. My typical boat wear consisted of shorts, T-shirts, and flip-flops, but that seemed disrespectful. And my hair wasn't helping matters either. The sleek beauty-salon look was gone, replaced by the usual frizz. Sure, the frizz had a better shape to it, but it was still frizz.

I ended up opting for a navy-blue sundress, a cotton pashmina draped over my shoulders, and my dressy flip-flops. Yes, there really is such a thing as dressy flip-flops, at least here in Florida. Scooter scrubbed up nicely—he had freshly ironed khaki pants on, which were paired with a dark-green button-up shirt and his deck shoes.

Confession time—we didn't own an iron or an ironing board. Given the lack of space we had on board our boat, they were luxury items that didn't make the cut, much like a Cuisinart. We didn't even have a place to hang clothes. Everything was stacked on shelves in a cupboard. Fortunately, we didn't have a full-length mirror either, so when we got dressed in the morning, we had no idea how bad we looked. It was a blessing in disguise. When you ate as many sugary treats as I did, it was nice not knowing exactly how big your behind really appeared in your shorts.

The only reason that Scooter was wrinkle-free for the memorial service was that Nancy took pity on him and offered to iron his outfit. That was the thing about her—she had these moments of thoughtfulness that made you forget all those other moments of crankiness, at least for a little while.

We headed to the public docks at the waterfront park to board the boat that would be taking the group out into the bay for the ceremony. I was impressed with how Norm had transformed his run-of-the-mill charter boat into a charming setting to celebrate Emily's short life. Ropes of greenery were tied around the railings with bows, yellow rose petals were scattered on the deck, and there was a framed picture of the young woman displayed in the main cabin flanked by those flameless candles that wouldn't burn the boat down if they fell over.

Jeff stood at the top of the boarding ramp, greeting everyone as they came on board. He looked terrible—dark circles under his eyes, ashen skin, and trembling hands. Even his misshapen ear seemed larger than normal.

In addition to Norm and his nephew, Liam, who was helping crew the boat, approximately fifteen people were in attendance. I looked around and saw Ned and Nancy sitting on a bench in the stern, their clothes ironed to perfection. I was pleased to see Penelope carrying trays laden with hors d'oeuvres and miniature cupcakes down below. Ever since the residents of Coconut Cove realized that Penelope had been the intended murder victim, business at her bakery had picked back up. Jeff had arranged for her to cater the memorial service, which I thought was touching, considering the circumstances of Emily's death.

I heard Penny's Texan twang before I

saw her. She was at the bow chatting with Ben. I was impressed with how well he had cleaned up. Tidy shorts and a shirt with a collar. Even his normally greasy hair was freshly washed, and there was a noticeable absence of grease stains on his hands.

Mike was standing on the dock, pacing back and forth and talking on his phone. After a few moments, he ended the call and gave Jeff a thumbs-up before he hoisted himself on deck. I groaned as I saw Chief Dalton shaking his hand. Just what we needed, Mr. No Comment on board. Then I saw him go over to Penelope and whisper something in her ear. That's when it hit me—the burly man was here to protect her. A sober reminder that the murderer was still on the loose.

"Did you see Alan?" Scooter asked as he handed me a glass of white wine. "He looks, um…"

I caught the photographer out of the

corner of my eye. "I can't believe he went through with it." The mild-mannered man waved before snapping a picture of us. Despite the fact that he was wearing his usual ensemble of gray clothes, which normally caused him to blend into the background, today he stood out for the wrong reasons. His formerly gray hair was now chestnut.

"Is that one of those DIY men's hair dyes?" Scooter asked.

"No, I think he paid good money at the salon for his new look." I watched as Alan flitted around the deck, chatting with people. He was exuding confidence, and every word he said could be heard clearly. No more mumbling. I shrugged. "Maybe it was a wise investment. He certainly seems to be feeling good about himself."

Scooter ran his fingers through his hair. "Do you think I need to color mine? Between the gray hairs and my beer belly, I'm beginning to look like my father."

"First of all, you don't have a beer belly. You're just a little bloated, and that's from all the rutabaga. And second, you only have a few gray hairs on your temples, and it makes you very distinguished looking. I always thought your father was a handsome man, and you are too."

"All right, folks," Norm said. "We're going to get under way."

Liam was untying the dock lines when a woman came rushing up. "Wait for me!"

"Is that Wanda?" I asked. "Shouldn't she still be in the hospital recovering?"

After the woman had clambered on board, Alan made a beeline for her. "How dare you blame me for what happened to you!" Wanda shrank back against the railing. "I was out of town at a wedding when you were poisoned. Ask the chief. He can back me up."

Penelope came to Wanda's rescue.

"Why don't you come down below and sign the memorial book?"

As the two ladies walked away, Alan shouted, "You haven't heard the last of this!" Who knew that hair dye could completely transform someone's personality.

* * *

The conditions were perfect—no wind and calm seas. Norm motored the boat across Sunshine Bay and dropped anchor in a quiet cove. Jeff stood at the bow while everyone gathered on deck. "I want to thank you all for coming this evening. It means a lot to me. One of the things that's impressed me ever since I moved to Coconut Cove is how kind, caring, and supportive everyone is. I know that Emily would be touched to see this turnout." He pressed his hand to his lips, gazed up at the sky, and blew a kiss. "I know that she's up there looking down at us…"

His voice cracked as tears formed in the corners of his eyes. Mike clasped his shoulder before handing him a napkin. "Thanks, mate," he said. After dabbing at his eyes, he took a deep breath. "I was so lucky to have been married to Emily, even if it was for a short time."

The crowd started murmuring. "Did he say married?" I whispered to Penny. "I thought they were engaged. He introduced her to me as his fiancée, not his wife, when you were showing them boats."

"It's news to me," she said. "Do you think they eloped?"

"When would they have had time to do that before her death?"

Scooter nudged me. "Shush. He's still talking."

Jeff was holding up the framed picture of Emily. "Would anyone like to come up and say a few words about my beloved wife?"

There was an uncomfortable silence as everyone looked at each other. Truth be told, no one had really known her.

Ned came to the rescue. "I suppose I could say a few words. I first met Emily when Penny brought her into the marina office to introduce her. She was a sweet young woman, always very polite. She seemed very interested in Coconut Cove, asking questions about what it was like to live in a small town on the mainland. And, um…she was, um—"

Nancy chimed in. "She was punctual."

"She was?" Ned asked.

"Yes. One day she said she'd be by the office at three in the afternoon to pick up some papers, and she was there at three on the dot." Nancy frowned. "Oh, wait a minute. I think that was another young woman. Never mind."

Ned looked flummoxed. Then he raised his glass. "Here's to Emily."

"I knew Emily better than anyone here," Alan said as he pushed his way forward to the front of the boat. "In fact, I took the photograph that Jeff's holding. See that smile on her face? She was smiling at me."

"Listen, mate," Jeff said, fury burning in his eyes. "She married me, not you. Understand?"

The rest of their conversation was drowned out when Norm started up the engine. "The sun is going to go down soon," he said while Liam pulled up the anchor. "We're going to head out to sea now so Jeff can scatter Emily's ashes as the sun sets."

While everyone stayed on deck sipping wine and gossiping about Jeff and Alan's altercation, I went down below to use the head. As I was washing my hands, I heard the door to the adjacent cabin creak open.

"Where did you put them, mate?" That was definitely Jeff.

"The urn is in that bag in the corner," the other man replied. He sounded like Mike.

"Okay, I see it now. What about the paperwork?"

"My guy is going to deliver it when the boat docks," Mike said.

"And it looks legit?" Jeff asked.

"That's why you paid extra. No one will ever be able to tell it apart from the real thing."

"It better work or I'm taking you down with me."

"No need to threaten me. I had enough of that from old man Van der Byl."

"Fine, you're right," Jeff replied. "It must be the stress of it all. Why don't you give me a few minutes to get myself together, and I'll join you back on deck?"

By this point, I was getting very uncomfortable. Bathrooms on boats can be very cramped, and the one on Norm's boat was no exception. I had wedged myself in between the tiny sink and a towel rack, but my right leg was beginning to fall asleep. Hopefully, Jeff would leave soon so I could sneak out without him seeing me.

"There you are," a woman said. "We need to talk."

Great, just what I needed. Another tête-à-tête with Jeff while I stayed in hiding, wondering what it was about marine toilets that made them smell so bad.

"What are you doing here, Wanda?" Jeff asked.

"You didn't think I'd miss out on saying goodbye to her, did you? I've known her for longer than you have." She began sobbing.

"Give me a break. You haven't spoken with her since she was a child."

Wanda blew her nose. "That doesn't mean she still wasn't special to me." The tone of her voice turned steely. "It's awfully convenient that you and Emily were married, isn't it? Especially as it means you've inherited everything. No need to eliminate any other…um, what's the best way to describe it… competition?"

"Just keep your mouth shut, do you hear me?" Jeff hissed.

"Sure, just as long as the monthly payments from the estate continue."

"You greedy little—"

Before Jeff could finish his thought, Liam came down to tell him that the sun was about to set. After a discreet interval, I opened the door and sneaked up onto deck. When I got there, Jeff was leaning over the stern rail, scattering Emily's ashes while the soundtrack to *Mamma Mia!* played in the background.

"Where have you been?" Scooter whispered as he handed me a memorial program. The front featured a picture of Emily, the same as the framed one that Jeff had been holding earlier. She really had been an attractive girl, I thought.

Long dark hair, striking green eyes, flawless bone structure...wait a minute, something was so familiar. What was it? Then it hit me—Emily was a younger version of Wanda. The similarities were unmistakable. They must have been related, but how?

Wanda had roots on Destiny Key before she had moved to Coconut Cove twenty-five years prior. Emily had lived on Destiny Key. Wanda had mentioned how her sister had committed suicide after she found out that her husband had had an affair, leaving a four-year-old daughter behind. Could Emily have been Wanda's niece? Could what she had written in her journal have been about the present-day death of Emily and not about what had happened in the past as she had previously told me? If so, and Emily had been killed by mistake, did that mean Wanda had meant to kill Penelope? What was the connection between the three women?

And who had poisoned Wanda, and why?

CHAPTER 16
POISONING IS SO EXHAUSTING

I tried to get a few quiet moments with Chief Dalton as the boat made its way back to Coconut Cove, but he rebuffed me. "Now's not the time or the place, Mrs. McGhie," he said. "But I promise you, I'll speak with you and your husband once we're back on shore."

"Scooter? Why do you want to speak with him?" I asked.

The burly man's reply was what you would have expected: "No comment."

Since he was being so uncooperative,

I decided to tackle Wanda instead. She was the key to it all. I had a hunch that if I could figure out exactly what her relationship to Emily had been and how Penelope factored into things, then I'd be able to solve the case.

Of my four original suspects, I had more or less ruled Alan out. While there certainly was a dark side to him that one rarely saw, I wasn't convinced that he would have attempted to kill Penelope merely because she didn't want to date him. He was also in the clear when it came to the poisoning of Wanda. If his wedding photography alibi hadn't been watertight, the chief wouldn't be letting him run around loose.

Mike was obviously a sleazy lawyer, but he didn't appear to have any reason to want Penelope dead. However, he did know the details of the Van der Byl estate, which could shed light on things. I made a mental note to try to worm that information out of him later. He had seemed ready to share some juicy details while Scooter and I were eating ice cream, but the discovery of Wanda collapsed on the ground had proved to be an untimely interruption.

That left me with Jeff and Wanda. In my gut, I knew that one of them had done it.

Here's the problem with my gut. It's very good at telling me when I'm hungry, and it's very good at nudging my intuition in the right direction. What it's bad at is follow-through. It sparks ideas in my head, but then it stops providing me with useful information and instead goes back to whining about the lack of potato chips and Hershey's Kisses in its life.

I'd say things like, *Gut, how could Wanda be the killer, as she herself was poisoned?* And it would reply in a low, gravelly voice, *Hungry! Very, very hungry!* Then I'd try something like, *Gut, why would Jeff want to kill Penelope?*

What's in it for him? And then I'd get another unhelpful reply: *Feed me! Feed me now!*

Darn it. I was going to have to sort this out by myself, no thanks to my annoying gut. I needed to get the killer to confess. It was that simple. I'd start with Wanda, see if I could get her to break. If not, then I'd move on to Jeff.

* * *

People are more likely to confess if they've had some wine, right? Makes sense to me. So I brought a glass of a lovely zinfandel, filled almost to the brim, over to Wanda. She was sitting by herself up at the bow.

"How are you holding up?" I asked. "You must be exhausted. Poisoning would do that to a person, wouldn't it? Exhaust them, right?"

Wanda took a healthy slug of her wine. "Poisoning is a little more serious than that. I could have died."

I felt my face grow warm. *Poisoning was exhausting*—what a stupid thing to say. "You were lucky that little girl found you when she did." There, that sounded better, didn't it?

"I really was," she replied, guzzling down more wine.

"Poor Emily. If only I had found her sooner." Wanda gave me a pained stare. "You were related, weren't you?" I asked gently.

She emptied her glass. "How did you know?"

"I didn't until I saw you next to her picture. The resemblance is uncanny."

"You should have seen her mother." She wrapped her arms around herself. "We looked so much alike. There were times people couldn't tell us apart."

"So Emily was your niece?"

Wanda twisted her body and rested her head on the rail, staring vacantly out at the water. "Yes, she was."

"Why did you pretend like you didn't know her?"

"I didn't have a choice." She glanced at her empty glass, then leaned toward me. "That's not entirely true. I did have a choice. A choice between money and family. I chose money."

"What do you mean?" I asked.

"After my sister killed herself, I threatened to expose him. To tell everyone about his affair. It would have ruined his social standing on Destiny Key." Her eyes narrowed as she spat out her words. "And he couldn't have that. No, not him. He wrote me a check, put me on the next ferry to the mainland, told me never to return and never to contact Emily, otherwise I'd be penniless. The checks kept coming and I kept silent."

The night had turned cool after the sun had set. I shivered in the light breeze. Wrapping my pashmina tightly around my body, I considered what

Wanda had said. Had the money she'd accepted from her brother-in-law been worth being separated from her niece?

Scooter poked his head out of the pilot house. "Are you two ladies okay out there? Why don't you come inside with the rest of us? Penelope's serving cupcakes and coffee."

"You're having a cupcake?" I asked.

"Jeff's been telling us about Emily's sweet tooth," Scooter said. "The cupcakes are in her memory. I couldn't really refuse, could I?"

Wanda's eyes welled up with tears. "Think of all the birthday cakes I missed as she was growing up," she said quietly.

I squeezed her hand, then turned to my husband. "I think we're going to stay out here. Save me a cupcake, though."

"Okay. Norm says we'll be docking in about twenty minutes."

"It's ironic that Penelope provided the cupcakes for Emily's memorial," Wanda said between sniffles.

"How exactly does she fit into all this?" I asked.

"I'm surprised you haven't figured it out," Wanda said. "You seem to have figured everything else out."

"Hmm, let's see. Your sister was twenty-five when she, um, passed away. And Emily was four at the time." Wanda nodded. "Her death would have been shortly after she found out that her husband's mistress was pregnant, right?"

"That's correct. She suspected he had been cheating on her for a while, but it wasn't until one of the nurses at the local clinic let it slip that the young woman who ran the bookmobile was expecting a child that the penny dropped. That's when she realized he was the child's father. He had been the one to set up the bookmobile program. Living on a small, out-of-the-way island meant that many of the residents didn't have access to a library. So he donated money to buy an old bus, had it refitted for use as a mobile library, and hired a young woman from the mainland to run it. He spent most of his free time helping her out, and one thing led to another."

"And that young woman was Penelope's mother," I said.

Wanda took a deep breath, then exhaled slowly. "Yes, she was."

"So that means Penelope and Emily were half sisters." Wanda nodded. "Did they know they were sisters?"

"As far as I know, Penelope never knew. Her mother did the same thing I did, accepted his blood money. She got checks every month, just like me."

"You must have resented her," I said. "Blamed her for your sister's death."

Wanda pursed her lips. "If it hadn't been for her, everything would have been fine!" she snapped. "I would have stayed on Destiny Key, watching my niece grow up and spending time with my sister. Instead, I spent the past twenty-five years stuck in Coconut Cove."

"That doesn't make sense," I said. "Why would you move to the same town as the woman you despised?"

"It was part of the terms he set me. I had to stay and keep an eye on Penelope and her mother. My brother-in-law figured if the two of us saw each other on a regular basis around town, we'd be reminded to keep our silence so we could keep our checks coming."

I considered my next words carefully. "It must have galled you to see Penelope grow up into a successful young woman when you were separated from your own niece. Perhaps enough to want to kill her?"

"I can see why you'd think that, but it wasn't me. I'm color-blind. The killer would have to be sure he poisoned the right slice of cake, and he would only be able to do that if he could be sure the plate was purple."

"I thought color-blindness only affected men," I said.

"Usually, but there's a small percentage of women who are affected. It has to do with genetics."

I felt another headache coming on. Instead of a math-induced one, this one felt science-related. I tried to remember what I had learned in my genetics class in high school, but all that came to mind were the letters X and Y and something to do with pea plants. Ugh. Peas. Such an overrated vegetable, much like rutabagas. As I mentally ranked vegetables in my head by order of tastiness (potatoes topped the list, especially in the form of french fries), I realized that there was something different about Wanda tonight.

"How come you're not wearing anything with Trixie Tremblay's face on it?" I asked.

"Let's just say we've parted ways."

"No more Rutamentals?"

"If I never see another rutabaga again in my life, it won't be soon enough," she said with a shudder.

"Wow," I said. "That's quite a turnaround. Do you mind having a word with Scooter and convincing him that rutabagas aren't all they're cracked up to be?"

"All you have to tell him is that if he keeps up with Rutamentals, he'll end up in the hospital like me."

I sat up straight. "Wait a minute, you mean you weren't poisoned?"

"No, it was a side effect of the rutabagas. Apparently, if you eat too many, you can develop some nasty symptoms, like a severe stomachache. It exacerbated my heart condition, which made it hard to breathe, causing me to lose consciousness."

"But why did you tell me that Alan had poisoned you?"

She bit her lip. "He'd been digging into

my background, and I was afraid he'd expose our family history."

"So you would have sent an innocent man to jail just to keep your dirty laundry from being aired?"

"I regret what I did," she said. "When you've spent your whole life lying and covering up lies, it becomes easy—all too easy—to keep lying."

"Did you tell the chief that you accused Alan falsely?"

"No, but what does it matter, anyway? He had an alibi for that day, and it turns out it wasn't poison, just too many rutabagas."

"It does matter. The poor man was dragged into the police station, questioned, and made to feel like a common criminal. Actually, worse than a common criminal. You implied he was a murderer." Wanda stared at the deck silently. "You knew he wasn't the murderer, didn't you?" She nodded. "You know who the murderer is, don't you?" She nodded again. "And before you found out it was the rutabagas that made you sick, you actually believed someone had tried to poison you, didn't you? You thought it was Jeff, right?"

Before she could answer, Norm called out, "Liam, get those dock lines ready. We're almost there."

While Norm maneuvered the boat toward the dock, Wanda grabbed my hands and stared at me intently. "I've said all I can," she said softly. "The chief knows Emily and I were related and he knows about Penelope, but he doesn't know everything. Talk to Mike. He can fill in the missing pieces. Talk to him before someone ends up taking the fall for Emily's murder."

* * *

Once the boat was secured, Wanda rushed off, pushing others out of her way in her haste.

"Is she feeling sick again?" Scooter asked. "She probably shouldn't have been discharged from the hospital so soon."

"She's sick because of rutabagas. And guilt…" my voice trailed off as I watched Mike help Penelope down to the dock.

"Guilt?" Scooter asked. "She feels guilty about rutabagas?"

"It's a long story. But I need to speak with Mike first. In the meantime, stay away from rutabagas. They really are bad for your health." I started to walk toward the lawyer when Scooter grabbed my arm. "Hey, you can't just run off like that without filling me in on what's going on."

"I'll be fine. Mike isn't the murderer."

"Right," Scooter said slowly. "So Mike isn't the murderer, and that makes it okay? Let me hazard a guess—you're planning on talking to him about murder, though."

"Of course. From what Wanda said,

he's the key to it all."

"Okay, no. Just no," Scooter said emphatically. "You're not going off to talk with someone about murder late at night by yourself. I'm coming with you."

"I'm afraid you aren't going anywhere, sir," an officious voice said, a voice that could belong to only one person—Chief Dalton. "I need to speak with you about some developments in the case," the burly man said.

"Don't you mean you need to speak with me?" I asked. "I'm the one who knows about the case."

"No, I need to speak with Mr. McGhie."

"Who you need to speak with is Jeff. He's the one who killed Emily."

"Emily wasn't the target," the chief said.

"I know that. We all know that," I said. "He meant to kill her sister, Penelope."

Scooter furrowed his brow. "Her sister? Penelope and Emily were sisters? How come I didn't know that?"

"As I told you, I have a lot to fill you in on." I turned to the chief. "But you knew they were related, didn't you?" His only reply consisted of raising one of his eyebrows. "Jeff thought he was killing Penelope. I just haven't figured out why yet, but I'm sure it has something to do with their father's estate."

"Maarten van der Byl's estate?" Scooter asked. "So this is all about money?"

"So you're admitting you knew Mr. Van der Byl?" the chief asked.

"I never met him personally. Everything was done through lawyers," Scooter said.

"But your company had dealings with him, isn't that correct?"

Scooter ran his fingers through his hair. "What does that have to do with anything?"

"That's exactly what we're going to find out. Now, if you wouldn't mind, I'll give you a ride to the police station."

"What?" I stepped forward and jabbed my finger at the chief. "Listen here, Tiny. You need to back off right now, and go arrest Jeff Morgan this instant!"

Scooter gently pulled me back. "Did you just call him Tiny?" he whispered in my ear.

The chief's face remained impassive. He pointed at his squad car. "Shall we, Mr. McGhie?"

"You can't question him without a lawyer," I said.

"I'm so tired of lawyers," Scooter said. "It seems like we can't do anything anymore without involving lawyers. And you can't trust any of them."

"That's not true. Some of them are trustworthy, like your lawyer, Tom. You've been working with him for years."

He sighed. "Fair enough. If only he wasn't laid up at the moment." He shook his head. "Listen, we're making a bigger deal out of this than we need to. I'm sure I can clear things up with Chief Dalton in no time. Nothing to worry about. I just want to get this over with as soon as possible. Why don't you go back to the boat, feed Mrs. Moto her supper, then come pick me up in our car." He turned to the chief. "It shouldn't take more than twenty minutes, a half hour tops, right?"

The chief shrugged.

"I can interpret his silence for you," I said to Scooter. "What he meant to say was 'no comment.'"

As the squad car sped away, I sank down on one of the park benches next to the public docks. Thoughts raced through my head—why did the chief want to question Scooter? He didn't really think he had anything to do with Emily's death, did he?

"Good night, Mollie," someone said behind me. I turned and saw Alan walking across the grass holding his camera. *Oh, no, the camera! That's what caused this all!* Scooter had been caught on tape near Penelope's table retrieving that kid's ball on the day of the cake competition. The chief would have taken one look at that and determined that Scooter had an opportunity to kill Emily. But the big question was, what motive did he think he had?

Mrs. Moto's dinner was going to have to wait. I had some investigating to do, starting with Mike.

CHAPTER 17
A BOX OF KITTENS

"Hey, wait a minute!" I stepped in front of Mike's car before he could pull out of the parking lot.

He rolled down the window and leaned out. "You could have been killed. I almost didn't see you."

"Killed. That's a good choice of words." I walked around to the passenger side, opened the door, and slid into the seat.

"Uh, what are you doing?" Mike asked.

"We're going to have a little chat."

He glanced at his watch. "Can this wait until tomorrow? I'm beat."

"No, it most certainly cannot. Scooter needs our help. He's at the police station. And you're going to get him out of that place."

"I can't represent him," he said, gripping the steering wheel. "But I can refer him to a criminal lawyer."

"He does need a lawyer, but it won't be one that you recommend. No, what I need from you is to know all the details of the Van der Byls' estate." Mike's phone buzzed. He reached for it, but I grabbed it from the dashboard before he could. "Hmm. Looks like a text from Jeff. Want me to read it out loud?"

"Give me that!" We tussled for a few moments, and then Mike gave up after I threatened to throw his phone out the window. He leaned back in his seat and groaned. "Has anyone ever told you how annoying you are?"

"Sure," I said with a shrug. "But the

people who usually say that are people who have something to hide. Like you. Look, I already know most of it. I just need you to fill in some of the details."

"What is it that you think you know?"

"One—Penelope is Maarten van der Byl's illegitimate daughter. Two—Emily and Penelope were half sisters," I said, ticking items off with my fingers. "Three —Wanda was Emily's aunt. Four— Maarten van der Byl bought Wanda's, as well as Penelope's mother's, silence. And five—Jeff is the murderer."

Mike ran his fingers through his hair. "If I tell you about the estate, will you leave me alone? Deal?"

"Let's hear what you have to say first, before I make any promises."

He shook his head and sighed. "Fine. Upon Maarten van der Byl's death, his estate was to be divided equally between his children."

I furrowed my brow. "If that's the case, how come Penelope doesn't know she was his daughter? Wouldn't you have had to inform her of her inheritance?"

"It's not that cut-and-dried. He didn't mention Penelope by name. The only way she would inherit was if she came forward with proof that she was his daughter."

"But she didn't know he was her father."

"Correct. And—"

"Oh, wait, I think I know what you're going to say next," I said. "Emily wanted to make sure that Penelope didn't know about her parentage. And with Penelope's mother having passed away, she would have never known unless someone else told her."

"That's right. And—"

"I know this one too!" I said, bouncing up and down in the car seat. It was like being on a game show, albeit one where the grand prize was saving your husband from incarceration. "The only people who knew about Penelope this whole time were Wanda and Emily."

"You're half-right," Mike said. "As you said before, Wanda had been paid off by Maarten van der Byl to keep quiet, but Emily didn't know about her sister until recently."

"Ah, that explains the interviews that Alan did with Wanda, Penelope, and Penelope's mom's friend."

Mike cocked his head to one side. "So you know about that."

I nodded. "Emily put Alan up to it, didn't she? She pretended to like him, going out on dates with him, but all she really wanted was for him to dig into Penelope's background."

"That's right. She ran across some old letters in her father's study and realized her father had another child. She just needed proof of who that child was, and then..." his voice trailed off when his phone buzzed again.

"Once she had the proof, she decided to eliminate her rival heir." I glanced at

Mike's phone. It was another text from Jeff: *When are you dropping off the papers?* I tapped my fingers on the screen. "No, that's not quite right. Emily didn't want to kill Penelope, did she? It was Jeff."

Mike stared out the windscreen and stroked his goatee. "I don't want to talk about Jeff."

"Why? Are you afraid he'll kill you too?"

"Kill me? No, he doesn't have any reason to. He has other ways of getting what he wants."

"But you are saying he's a murderer."

He shook his head. "I'm not saying any such thing. But if we're talking hypothetically, Jeff isn't a violent person by nature. He doesn't even own a gun."

"You don't need a gun to kill someone. Turns out poison is pretty effective."

"Let's just say that was a one-off." He held up his hands. "Hypothetically, of course. People like Jeff and the Van der

Byls are more sophisticated when it comes to getting what they want. Blackmail, forged documents, less-than-legitimate legal transactions, financial fraud—those are their tools of the trade."

"He has something on you, doesn't he?" The lawyer nodded. "But he didn't have anything on Penelope, so he had to resort to poison, right?"

Mike drummed his fingers on the steering wheel. "I've said all that I'm going to say. We had a deal. Once I told you about the estate, you promised to leave me alone." He leaned across me and opened the passenger door. "You should probably go see what's happened to your husband."

I reluctantly exited the car. As I walked toward my own car, Mike pulled up alongside me, leaned out the window and held out his hand. "You've still got my phone."

"Just one more question," I said.

"Wouldn't Jeff still want Penelope dead? Otherwise, he only inherits the half of the estate that belonged to Emily."

"But Emily and Jeff were married," Mike said. "That changes everything. In the event that Emily married within a year after her father's death, she stood to inherit the entire estate. Don't worry, Penelope is safe now. So are you and everyone else. Jeff has all his ducks in a row."

I dropped the phone into his hand and watched him speed away. While Mike had answered a lot of questions, he hadn't answered all of them. And I needed answers, not only to put a killer behind bars but also to save my husband from being falsely accused.

* * *

I didn't have time to get answers to my questions, not with Scooter at the police station. I rushed over there, breaking speed limits willy-nilly, only to end up waiting on the hard wooden bench in the lobby for hours.

The receptionist was pleasant the first twenty times I asked her how much longer my husband would be. After that, her only response was "no comment." She even had the nerve to pretend to be on the phone when I asked her if I could have one of the donuts she had in the box next to her computer.

I tried to forget about my hunger pangs by texting my mom.

You were joking about Mary, right?

No response. I tried again.

Do I need to worry about my ears becoming unnaturally large?

Crickets. Maybe she was playing bridge. I spent the next thirty minutes reorganizing the contents of my purse. I really did have a lot of pens. Finally, my phone buzzed.

I would never make fun of you. It's so cute when kids have imaginary friends.

Or a twin sister, in your case.

I ran my fingers through my hair, then tapped a reply.

OMG. Did you mean Veronica this whole time?

Wasn't her name Mary?

No. Veronica. Not even close.

Oops. Gotta go. Got brownies in the oven.

I could really have used a brownie by this point. Texting with my mom always drove me nuts and straight into sugar's open arms. I stared up at the ceiling and smiled, remembering Veronica. Sometimes, it had been lonely being an only child when I was younger. Making up an imaginary sister had helped.

I slapped my thighs. Shoot. While the mystery of Mary was solved, my mom hadn't answered the really important question. I sent her one last text.

What about my ears?

Not surprisingly, I didn't hear back. Like me, when my mom is focused on brownies, everything else fades into the background, including the sound of a phone buzzing.

My stomach churned as I watched the hours tick by on the large clock mounted on the wall. I paced back and forth, stopping periodically to reread the wanted posters, reward notices, and takeout menus tacked to the bulletin board. I had tried in vain to have Thai food delivered to the station, but the restaurant had already closed.

The reward notices were typical of crime in Coconut Cove—information was sought about the theft of a golf cart from the Tropical Breeze condos, the identity of the person who had left a box of ten-week-old kittens outside the Tipsy Pirate (they had all since been adopted), who was passing counterfeit ten-dollar bills around town, and who had stolen roses from Mrs. MacDougal's garden.

While I was staring at the wanted

posters and wondering what would compel someone to get a tattoo on their face, the door to the interior of the station swung open. Scooter stood there in a daze. He looked awful. His previously freshly ironed clothes were now wrinkled, his face was drawn, and his eyes were bloodshot.

"What did they do to you?" I asked as I hugged him.

"They asked me a lot of questions, over and over." He pulled back and brushed my hair behind my ears. "Mollie, it doesn't look good. I think I'm in real trouble."

My heart sank. The only time Scooter ever called me by my first name instead of by a pet name was when things were serious. "What's going on?"

"They think I murdered Emily."

I gasped. "The chief said that?"

"Not in so many words."

"Well, what words did he use? I know Chief Dalton isn't prone to verbosity, but he must have said something."

Scooter tucked his shirt into his pants. "He kept asking me about Emily and Penelope, about the Van der Byl estate, and about my business ties to them. Then he mentioned a cousin of Maarten van der Byl, some guy named Andreas."

"Who's that?"

"I met him once at a telecommunications conference. We had a drink together. He has a different last name, so I didn't connect him with the Van der Byl family. But apparently, if both Emily and Penelope are out of the picture, then Andreas is next in line to inherit the bulk of the estate."

"So what does that have to do with you?"

"The chief thinks I want Andreas to be running the Van der Byl business, because he would make all the contract disputes go away. Can you believe he thinks I would murder an innocent young woman to save my business?"

He pulled me into a bear hug. "I'm so glad I have you by my side."

I squeezed him back. "Always," I said. "I'll always be by your side."

"Now, how about something to eat?" Scooter asked. "I'm starved."

"I think everything is going to be closed by now except a fast food place."

"That sounds good to me. The greasier the better." He opened up his wallet. "I think I might even have a coupon in here." He pulled out a stack of bills and shuffled through them. "There it is. A free chocolate milkshake with the purchase of a burger."

As he started to shove the cash back in his wallet, I stopped him. "Let me see those ten-dollar bills." I pointed at the notice on the bulletin board. "There's some counterfeit money being passed around. We should get these checked."

Then it hit me—people who counterfeited money needed to make it look as genuine as possible so they didn't get caught. The same thing went for forged documents. If you wanted something to pass scrutiny, you had to pay extra, and you had to know someone who could arrange for that sort of thing. Someone like Mike. Ten to one, Jeff's wedding certificate to Emily was a fake. Now, I just had to prove it.

* * *

The next morning, I let Scooter sleep in. He had tossed and turned for hours before finally falling into a deep slumber. I hadn't slept well either. My nightmares had taken on new proportions. How I longed for the day when only rutabagas and raccoons haunted my dreams, instead of visions of my husband languishing in a jail cell.

Mrs. Moto knew something was amiss. She didn't yowl as usual for her breakfast when the sun came up.

Instead, she stayed perched on top of Scooter's pillow, keeping watch over him.

After leaving a note saying I'd be back soon with breakfast, I grabbed my bag and sneaked off the boat. I made a couple of phone calls to ensure everything was set up, and then I headed to the waterfront park for my meeting. You'll notice I didn't say I stopped off for a coffee or pastry beforehand. That's how serious things were—stopping for caffeine or sugar wasn't an option.

After parking my car, I walked over to the sports pavilion. The place was deserted, something I was counting on. I pushed the door open and walked inside. The room looked exactly like it had on the day of the cake competition. The cakes, plates, and tablecloths had been removed, but the setup was the same, even down to the barrier dividing the place into two and the Trixie

Tremblay posters on the walls.

I sat behind one of the tables in the back and waited. After a few minutes, the door opened and Jeff walked in.

"Thank you for coming here," I said, my voice shaking slightly. I knew I was taking a calculated risk meeting Jeff, but, based on what Mike had told me, I didn't think the Aussie would try to kill me. The lawyer had said everyone was safe from Jeff, including me. My assumption was that this meant that if he did try anything, it would involve something nonlethal, like blackmail.

Jeff sat in the chair across from me. "My pleasure, mate. I figure we should clear a few things up."

"I know about the wedding certificate. It's a fake. Mike arranged for it to be forged so you could pretend that you and Emily had been married all along."

"You're a clever girl, aren't you?" he said with a sneer.

"Not clever enough," I said. "If I was,

then Scooter wouldn't have been questioned by the police. You'd be in jail instead."

Jeff leaned back in his chair and put his arms behind his head. "About that. I think your husband is going to have to spend some more time in jail."

I leaned forward. "I don't think so. You're the one going to jail. Once the chief finds out about your fake wedding, it will all be over."

"Well, here's the thing. He isn't going to find out. It's your word against mine. Besides, Mike's guy is an expert in what he does. No one is going to think my wedding certificate is fake."

"That piece of paper might work at first, but all they have to do is check the state records. There's no way you could have hacked into the government systems too."

"Ah, you're not as clever as you think, are you? The wedding certificate isn't from Florida. It's from a small Caribbean island, one where government officials are more than happy to look the other way with the right enticement."

"You mean a bribe?"

He put his finger on his nose. "Bingo!"

"Bribe or not, people are still going to question it. All this time, you've been saying that you were just engaged. Now, you've changed your story, and you're claiming she married you."

"That's easily explained. You see, Emily flew down to the islands with me to a pharmaceutical conference a couple of weeks ago. We got swept away with the romance of it all and were secretly married. It was a beautiful ceremony. It took place at sunset on the beach. Emily had flowers in her hair and wore a white sundress. I wore a white shirt and Bermuda shorts. We were both barefoot. After the justice of the peace pronounced us husband and wife, I drew a heart in the sand with our initials inside of it." He smirked. "Romantic, huh? People are going to lap that story up when I tell them."

I had to admit, it did sound romantic. Except for the part about it being a total fake. "How are you going to explain the fact that neither of you told anyone about it?"

He shrugged. "Easy. She wanted to have a formal reception on Destiny Key. That's when we'd announce we were already married. She thought it would be a fun surprise."

I chewed my lip. It did sound convincing. This man could talk anyone into anything. It probably explained his success as a sales rep. I steeled myself and got to the heart of the matter. "Couldn't you have been happy with half of the Van der Byl estate?" I asked. "Was it really worth murdering someone to get all of it? You killed your own fiancée, for goodness' sake."

Jeff frowned. "That was an unfortunate accident. I was fond of Emily. She rarely left the island, except for business. So when I met her at her lawyer's office in Miami, I figured it was meant to be. I was looking forward to marrying her. It was Penelope I wanted out of the way."

"Because you were afraid she would find out that she was Maarten van der Byl's daughter?" He nodded. "And you didn't have any way to blackmail her to keep her from claiming her share of the estate?"

"Correct." He leaned forward. "That girl's reputation is spotless. I couldn't find any leverage on her."

"So you admit it. You meant to kill Penelope."

"Sure, I admit it," he said. "I didn't have a choice. Sometimes, people get in the way."

"People like your former fiancée?"

Jeff furrowed his brow. "How do you know about her?"

"It's not important. What happened to her? Did you poison her too?"

"Let's just say she drank something she shouldn't have." He looked up at the ceiling for a few moments. "She really shouldn't have tried to make me sign a prenuptial agreement," he said softly.

I shifted in my seat. Jeff certainly wasn't holding anything back. I'd suspected that his arrogance would drive him to want to tell someone about how clever he had been. About how he managed to get exactly what he wanted, no matter what the cost to anyone else. My palms were clammy. Jeff's confession was coming a little too easily.

Never mind. Things had already gone this far. I had to press on. "Wanda knew about your former fiancée, didn't she? You were ensuring she still got regular payment from the estate, right?"

Jeff's eyes grew cold. "Hmm. Maybe I've underestimated you."

"Perhaps you should check to make sure no one is around when you have secret conversations."

He nodded slowly. "Fair enough."

"Maybe you can clear something up for me," I said. "When you and Wanda were talking outside the Sugar Shack the night Emily died, you said something about her having a vested interest in her death. What did you mean by that?"

"It all comes down to money. If Emily had been unmarried at the time of her death, Wanda would have inherited a modest sum, more than she's getting now with her monthly payments. But as we know, Emily was married to me, so Wanda gets nothing."

"Fake married, you mean."

"Like I said, it's your word against mine, and, well, my word is backed up with some very authentic looking paperwork." He leaned forward and placed his hands on the table. "Not that it matters, because here's what's going to happen. Your husband is going to confess to killing Emily."

I sat back in my chair. "Huh? Why would he do that?"

"To protect you, of course. You see, Mike's guy does an excellent job forging not only wedding certificates but also other things, like emails and letters. I have a file folder full of some very convincing evidence that you plotted to kill Penelope. You stole the bottle of gelsemium and poured it on Penelope's slice of cake, knowing that it would kill her. You'd do anything to save your husband's business." He smirked. "At least, that's what all the documents I have in my possession would lead anyone to believe."

"So just to be clear, you killed Emily, you faked your marriage to her, and you forged documents implicating me in Emily's death."

"That about sums it up. I've seen how the two of you are together. Your husband loves you very much. He'll do anything to keep you from going to jail.

The police already think he did it, so it's just a simple matter of his confession." Jeff pushed back his chair and stood. "I'll expect Scooter to turn himself in to the police by the end of the day."

As he sauntered out the front entrance, I took a deep breath and put my head in my hands. Then I walked to the back door and pushed it open. "Did you get all that?" I asked.

Alan held up his tablet. "It's all on here, saved to the cloud, and I just emailed a link to Chief Dalton."

"Okay, let's grab the camera, and then I'll treat you to a coffee."

I watched as Alan walked over to the Trixie Tremblay poster by the rear door, peeled it back, and pulled out a camera that had been wedged on a small ledge hidden behind Trixie's face. As he pressed the poster back in place, I smiled at how her right eye had been discreetly cut out with just enough room for the camera lens to peek through. For once in my life, I was grateful for Rutamentals.

CHAPTER 18
THE NEWEST YOUTUBE
SENSATION

"Wish us luck," I said. Mrs. Moto squirmed in my arms as I adjusted her costume.

Scooter scratched her head. "You don't need luck. The two of you look adorable. I think this is going to be the year that the first feline ever wins the Coconut Cove pet-costume competition."

Nancy's voice boomed over the loudspeaker. "Attention: all dog owners, and, ahem, cat owner, please bring your pets to the main stage immediately for the costume inspection."

"Costume inspection?" Scooter asked.

"She said something the other day about all costumes needing to be compliant. If they aren't, your pet is automatically disqualified."

Scooter examined the metallic belt wrapped around her middle. "You did an amazing job with this," he said. "Are you going to have her wear the hood up or down?"

"I think up when we first walk across the stage, then I'll pull it down to reveal what's underneath."

The loudspeaker boomed again. "Attention: this is your three-minute warning. All pet-costume competition entrants to the main stage immediately."

"You better get going," Scooter said, kissing us both on the top of our heads. "I need to go get set up with Alan."

"Set up for what?"

"He's going to film the competition. I want to watch and learn how he does it. He was telling me about his YouTube channel, and I was thinking we should start one for Mrs. Moto." Our calico meowed loudly. "See, I think she agrees."

"Well, the man to learn about making great videos from is definitely Alan."

"Isn't that the truth," Scooter said. "If it hadn't been for him taping Jeff's confession yesterday and sending it to Chief Dalton, I'd be in jail."

"Attention: Mollie McGhie. Please bring your feline to the stage immediately. This is your final warning."

"We better scoot," I said.

After barely passing the costume inspection—Ned intervened when Nancy wanted to eliminate us on the basis that she didn't know what Mrs. Moto was dressed as—we took our place backstage.

While our soon-to-be YouTube

sensation sat calmly in my arms purring, the dogs were running around sniffing each other and tangling up their leashes in the process. Their barking drowned out what Nancy was saying over the loudspeaker. Eventually, she poked her head behind the curtain and glared at humans and dogs alike. "Quiet!" Everyone obeyed immediately. "That's better. Now, I'm going to call you up one by one. Walk your dog or"—she paused and peered at me over her reading glasses—"your *feline* across the stage toward the podium. Stop for a moment while I read out the description of your pet's costume. Then promptly exit to the other side of the stage. Is that clear?"

The humans nodded, the dogs barked in unison, and Mrs. Moto meowed.

The first dog up was a chihuahua dressed as Superman. He was a fierce little thing. If attitude was one of the judging criteria, he would have won hands down. After a few more dogs took their turn, the German shepherd, Chica, made an appearance wearing a shark costume. An extremely energetic dog, she tore across the stage without pausing at the podium. Then she raced back to the other side, her human desperately trying to keep up.

"If you can't control your dog, it will be disqualified," Nancy said. Chica did what any dog would do in a situation like that. She walked over to Nancy, gazed at her with soulful eyes, then held out her paw. Nancy surprised everyone by shaking her paw. Hmm. Maybe she was a dog person after all.

Next up was Bob, the terrier who we all thought should run for mayor against Norm. He strutted across the stage in a Sherlock Holmes outfit. He appeared utterly dignified until someone in the audience threw a tennis ball on stage. There was nothing Bob liked more than chasing tennis balls, and there was nothing Nancy liked less than dogs dropping balls at her feet and expecting her to play fetch. After kicking the ball to the side and admonishing Bob's owners, she called out the next dog's name. Maybe she wasn't a dog person after all.

I wondered what she was going to make of the next contestant—Chloe, the chocolate Labrador retriever. She was dressed in a hula skirt and lei and carried a coconut in her mouth. When she got to the podium, she laid down on the ground and started husking the coconut. Her tail wagged from side to side as shredded coconut husk flew everywhere. I stifled a smile when I saw Nancy pluck some out of her hair with disdain. After a few minutes, Chloe picked the husked coconut up in her mouth, carried it to the edge of the stage, and deposited it in Penelope's hands. I had a feeling coconut pie was going to be on the menu at the Sugar Shack later that day.

"And now, join me in welcoming the winners of the pet-costume competition for three years in a row, Frick and Frack." I wished Anabel luck as she herded the Yorkies onto the stage. "Don't they look adorable dressed up as fairies?" Nancy asked the audience.

Finally, it was our turn. You know what they say—you save the best for last. Mrs. Moto walked confidently toward the middle of the stage. When we got to the podium, I picked her up and pulled back her hood. The audience gasped in delight when they saw what she had on her head.

"This is our feline entry," Nancy said with zero enthusiasm. "She's owned by Mollie and Scooter McGhie and—"

"Actually, it's the other way around," I interjected. "When it comes to cats, they own their humans."

Nancy tapped her perfectly manicured fingernails on the podium. "Are you done? Good. As I was saying, Mrs.

Moto is a Japanese bobtail cat who is modeling a"—she paused to adjust her reading glasses—"a Princess Leia costume. Who is Princess Leia? I've never heard of her before. I've heard of Princess Grace and Princess Diana, but Leia is new to me."

I turned to Nancy, holding my cat up. "Of course you know Princess Leia. Everyone knows who she is. This long white senatorial gown is the outfit from the original *Star Wars*. Surely, you recognize the earmuff hairstyle?"

The older woman shook her head, then straightened her papers on the podium. "You may exit the stage now. We'll begin our deliberations."

While the judges added up their scores, Mrs. Moto and I were surrounded by members of the audience, all eager to see the Princess Leia costume up close and take pictures. Alan and Scooter filmed the crowd, while our calico basked in the adoration.

"Attention: will all pet-costume competitors and their owners please return to the stage."

After Nancy made sure we were all neatly lined up, she opened the envelope that the judges had handed her. "In third place is Bob, the terrier who was dressed as Sherlock Holmes. In second place is Chloe, the chocolate Lab who was dressed up as a Hawaiian hula dancer."

"And now for the grand prize winner." While Nancy paused for dramatic effect, Anabel reached out and squeezed my hand. "No matter how it turns out, I just wanted to say I'm glad we've become friends." I squeezed her hand back and wished her and the Yorkies luck.

"The dog taking home this year's crown is...this can't be right." Nancy walked over to the judges and pointed at the results. After a lengthy consultation, she shook her head and returned to the podium. "This year's winner of the Coconut Cove pet-costume competition isn't a dog, it's the *feline*, Mrs. Moto."

"Way to go!" Scooter shouted. Mrs. Moto leaped out of my arms and darted to the front of the stage. The kids in the audience ran up and took turns congratulating her and scratching her belly. I sighed in relief. After everything we had been through over the past week, beginning with Emily's murder and ending with Scooter practically being accused of killing her, it was nice to have something finally go our way.

* * *

"Cupcakes for everyone," Penelope said as she set three large purple boxes on the table. An impromptu gathering had broken out after the pet-costume competition. The group had laid out blankets on the grass and commandeered the picnic tables and grill by the waterfront. Ned was dishing up hamburgers and hot dogs, while Nancy scooped potato salad and coleslaw on plates. To everyone's relief, there wasn't a single rutabaga in sight.

"Hey, those are for dessert," Scooter said when I tried to peek into the pastry boxes.

"So, what I hear you saying is that dessert is back on," I said as I slid onto the bench next to him.

"It is," he said as he squeezed some ketchup onto his burger. After he took a bite, he added, "But in moderation. It's possible I might have gone overboard with Rutamentals, but I still think my motivation was worthwhile. We really need to take better care of ourselves so we can Live Healthy, Live Long—"

"Yeah, yeah, I know—Live Strong." I ate some potato salad. It had the perfect mix of mayo and mustard. "Why don't we try to come up with an eating plan that works for both of us." I waved my fork at him. "But I have two rules. One— we have to be able to eat dessert and french fries at least twice a week." Scooter nodded. "And two—no rutabagas."

"What was the deal with all those rutabagas?" Penny asked as she sat down next to me.

"I think you were one of the few people in Coconut Cove who didn't get suckered into the Rutamentals diet," I said.

"There were some good aspects to it," Scooter said.

I smiled. "Wanda got sick from eating too many rutabagas. That certainly wasn't good."

"I thought she had been poisoned," Penny said.

"She thought she had been too, but it turned out not to be the case," I said. "You missed a lot while you were out of town."

"Where were you, anyway?" Ben asked.

"In Miami looking at some boats," she replied. "What else happened?" After I explained about how Jeff had plotted to kill Penelope so Emily would inherit all her father's estate, she shook her head. "I always thought there was something off about him."

"I know," I said. "His ears gave it away."

Penny laughed so hard that she almost choked on her hot dog. "His ears? Since when can you tell if someone is a murderer by their ears?"

"What was wrong with his ears?" Ben asked.

"Didn't you notice how one was misshapen and much larger than the other one? I couldn't take my eyes off it."

Ben shrugged. "Sounds like cauliflower ear."

"Huh? Do you get that from eating too

much cauliflower? Oh my gosh, what are the side effects of eating too many rutabagas? What's going to happen to Scooter? He ate a lot of them. Is one of his ears going to start growing?"

"Well, they do say your ears keep growing as you get older, like your nose, feet, and hands," Ben said. "But cauliflower ear comes from getting hit. Rugby's big down under. The guys get knocked around, and their ears get damaged."

Scooter sighed. "So, in addition to turning fifty and getting a beer belly and gray hair, now I have to worry about my nose, feet, and hands getting bigger?"

"Don't forget about the hair that will start growing uncontrollably from your ears," Penny added with a chuckle. "On a more serious note, how did you get Jeff to admit to what he had done?"

"That was easy. He was really full of himself, a real Mr. Know-It-All. I knew he would want to brag about how clever he was. Alan was happy to help. He set up a hidden camera in the sports pavilion and monitored everything from outside. I called Jeff and told him that I wanted to meet, set a time, then just sat back and listened to him confess."

"I still think you should have told me what you were up to," Scooter said. "Things might not have gone as smoothly as you planned. He could have turned on you."

"But he didn't," I said, giving Scooter a quick kiss on the cheek. "Everything worked out okay."

Penelope walked over to the table and opened the boxes. "Are you guys ready for a cupcake?"

"Me! Me! Can I have one of the chocolate ones?" I asked. After she passed me one on a napkin, I thanked her. Then I looked back and forth between the baker and the Texan sitting to my right. "What are the odds that the two of you would have the same name?"

Penny's brow furrowed. "What do you mean? Hers is Penelope and mine is Penny."

"Isn't Penny short for Penelope?" Scooter asked.

"Nope. It's just plain Penny. My mom found a penny on the sidewalk after the doctor told her that she was pregnant with me. You know the saying—'Find a penny, pick it up, and all the day, you'll have good luck.' She had been trying for years, so she took it as a sign that her luck had finally changed. When I was born, she named me Penny."

"That's sweet," I said. "Although it is a bit confusing at times having a Penelope and a Penny in the same town."

Ben wadded up his napkin on his plate and held out his hand for a cupcake. After Penelope doled out a few more to us (yes, I nabbed a second chocolate one), she walked over to the other table before we ate more than our share.

"What else did I miss?" Penny asked.

"A lot of family drama," Ben said as he wiped frosting off his mouth. "Turns out Penelope and Emily were sisters, and Wanda was Emily's aunt. There's some bad blood there."

"I'm not so sure about that." I watched as Penelope sat down on the picnic blanket next to Wanda and offered her a cupcake. "Penelope is too sweet of a person. I don't think she can stay angry with anyone for long or hold a grudge. Who knows, maybe the two of them might become friends over time."

"Penelope sure did dodge a bullet when Emily ate that cake instead of her," Ben said. "What was that stuff he put on it called again?"

"Gelsemium," I said. "Because Jeff was a pharmaceutical sales rep, he knew about the dangers of herbal medicines, especially if someone had a preexisting health condition. Thanks to the interviews Alan did on behalf of Emily, he knew Penelope had a heart condition. When he saw that bottle of gelsemium, he grabbed it and waited for the right opportunity to use it."

"And that was at the cake competition," Penny said.

"That's right. Unfortunately, Emily sneaked back to the sports pavilion to cut another slice of Jeff's cake while he was occupied watching the fire. Then she took the other slice out to the fishing pier and ate it. She had the same heart condition as her half sister, and the gelsemium ended up killing her."

Everyone was silent for a few minutes, lost in their thoughts.

"I've got more hot dogs and burgers," Ned called out from the grill. "Come and get 'em." Penny and Ben grabbed their plates and excused themselves. Scooter convinced me to skip seconds as part of our new approach to eating in moderation.

"Do you think she's bothering him?" my husband asked, pointing at Chief Dalton, who was sitting under a tree next to Anabel. The two Yorkies were sleeping in their doggie bed, and, much to my surprise, Mrs. Moto was dozing in the chief's lap while he stroked her.

"Can you pass me that hot dog you didn't finish?" I asked. "She's probably hungry. I'll go take her a snack."

All three of the critters woke up when I approached. The smell of grilled meat will do that to you. I knelt on the grass and handed out the treats. "One at a time," I said. "Frack, you're first. Now Frick. Okay, Mrs. Moto, now it's your turn." After the last piece was given out and my hands had been thoroughly licked clean by their tongues, I scratched the calico's head. "Are you bothering the chief and Anabel?"

"She's fine," the burly man said gruffly. "For some reason, Frick and Frack have taken a liking to her."

"Admit it, Tiny, you have too," Anabel said.

"Why exactly is your nickname Tiny?" I asked.

The chief raised one of his bushy eyebrows. "No comment." Then he turned to Anabel. "It's our little secret, right?"

"No comment," she replied with a smile. As she adjusted Frick's and Frack's fairy wings, she congratulated me on Mrs. Moto's costume and taking the top prize. Then she wagged her finger at me playfully. "But wait until you see what I have lined up for next year's costumes. We're going to take back the crown."

Alan walked toward us, his chestnut hair glimmering in the sunlight. "Can you all sit next to each other with the dogs and cat in the front?" he asked, holding up his camera.

After he was finished, the chief cleared his throat. "Good job," he said.

"Both of you."

Anabel leaned over and whispered in my ear, "Tiny rarely offers any praise. You two must have really impressed him."

I knew I should have left when the going was good, but I couldn't help myself. "It was actually the three of us. If Mrs. Moto hadn't found Wanda's journal, then I never would have followed the clues that led to discovering the tragic Van der Byl family history and uncovering Jeff's role in trying to make sure Emily inherited everything."

Mrs. Moto meowed in agreement while the chief scowled.

* * *

After the picnic, both Scooter and I were stuffed, despite not having seconds. Mrs. Moto, on the other hand, yowled until her dinner was served. After she gobbled down all her Frisky Feline Ocean's Delight, the three of us sat in the cockpit and watched the sun go down over the boatyard.

"I've got a surprise for you," I said to Scooter. "I signed us up for the Fourth of July regatta with the Coconut Crew. It's going to be great. We'll race up to Destiny Key and anchor overnight. Then there are shorter races and activities during the weekend, followed by a race back to Coconut Cove."

Scooter's mouth fell open. "Really, that's something you want to do? Even after *Naut Guilty* and *The Codfather II* crashed into each other?"

"What are the chances something like that could happen again? Statistically, it's not possible."

"I don't think I've ever heard you use mathematically based logic before," he said with a chuckle. "If you want to talk statistics, what are the chances you would have found five dead bodies since we've moved to Coconut Cove?"

"Okay, you may have a point." I toyed with my necklace while I considered what he said. After a few moments, I slapped my hands on my thighs. "You know what, math gives me a headache. Let's not think about statistics. Let's just go for it. Owning a boat has been your dream, and I loved racing on *Pretty in Pink*. It'll be fun to do some more sailing."

"The Fourth of July." Scooter chewed on his lip. "That's a little over three months away. Do you think we'll be ready by then? We've got a lot of boat projects left on our list."

"We'll have to be. The deposit was nonrefundable. Anyway, I've already checked one thing off the list—I sorted out our insurance policy. After what happened to Mike, I want to make sure that we're covered for racing." I held up my hands. "Not that we're going to crash into anyone, of course."

He nodded. "Okay, let's buckle down and get it done."

Mrs. Moto crawled into my lap and curled up in a ball. "I was thinking I should make her a little sailor's costume, complete with a captain's hat."

Scooter smiled. "Why don't you make three? That way the crew of *Marjorie Jane* can have matching outfits."

"Oh, I almost forgot. I have another surprise for you." I reached into a bag sitting on the bench next to me and pulled out a box. "Ta-da!"

"What is it? Is that cereal?"

"Yep. Since you're off Rutamentals, I figured it was time you got back to your regular diet. I know you used to eat Cap'n Crunch, but I got you Lucky Charms this time. After everything that happened with your business, I figured you could use a little luck."

Scooter sighed. "About that. I was thinking it might be time for a career change. I've got a few ideas in mind."

"Whatever you want to do, I'm behind you one hundred percent." I leaned against Scooter's chest and looked out at the boats in the yard. Soon we'd be leaving this place, putting *Marjorie Jane* back into the water where she belonged and taking her out sailing. What could possibly go wrong?

AUTHOR'S NOTE AND ACKNOWLEDGMENTS

Thank you so much for reading my book! If you enjoyed it, I'd be grateful if you would consider leaving a short review on the site where you purchased it and/or on Goodreads. Reviews help other readers find my books while also encouraging me to keep writing.

My experiences buying our first sailboat with my husband in New Zealand (followed by our second sailboat in the States), learning how to sail, and living aboard our boats inspired me to write the *Mollie McGhie Sailing Mysteries*. You could say that there's a little bit of Mollie in me.

Be on the lookout for the fourth book in the series, *Dead in the Dinghy.* You can sign up for my free newsletter for

updates on new releases at:
https://www.subscribepage.com/m4g9m4

I want to thank my wonderful beta readers who were so generous with their time, graciously reading earlier drafts and providing insightful and thoughtful feedback: Alexandra Palcic, Duwan Dunn, Elizabeth Seckman, Greg Sifford, and Liesbet Collaert.

I also want to thank Michele Dunn for her continual support and the great idea about being on a "live-it," rather than a diet.

Some of the adorable dogs who make an appearance in *Poisoned by the Pier* are based on boat dogs who I've met in real life. Chloe belongs to Doug Stephenson and Tina Riley (s/v Amazed), Bob belongs to Ted and Sandy Kearney (s/v Ragtime Gal), and

Chica belongs to Phil and Michelle Mavis (s/v Mariposa).

Most of all, I want to thank my husband, Scott Jacobson, for his encouragement throughout the writing process. Not only is he an amazing alpha reader and beta reader, he is also the inspiration behind many of the best bits in this book.

The followers of my blog, *The Cynical Sailor*, have been a huge source of inspiration. Their kind words and encouragement motivated me to publish my first book and continue writing. I've been fortunate to have made good friends (both virtual and in-person) through the blogging community.

As always, many thanks to Chris Brogden at EnglishGeek Editing for his keen eye, thoughtful edits, and support. He goes above and beyond the call of duty, for which I am very grateful.

And many, many thanks to all of my readers. Your support and encouragement means everything.

ABOUT THE AUTHOR

Ellen Jacobson is a writer who lives aboard a 34-foot sailboat, *s/v Tickety Boo*, with her husband and an imaginary cat named Simon. Her cozy mystery series, *The Mollie McGhie Sailing Mysteries,* featuring a reluctant sailor turned amateur sleuth, is inspired by her own sailing adventures and misadventures.

In addition to murder mysteries, she also enjoys writing sci-fi and fantasy stories. When she isn't killing off characters, creating imaginary worlds, working on boat projects, or seeking out deserted islands, she blogs about her travel adventures and daily life living aboard a sailboat at: thecynicalsailor.blogspot.com.

If you would like updates on current and

future releases, please see her website at: ellenjacobsonauthor.com.

You can also follow along on:

Twitter: @Ellen__Jacobson
Facebook: @EllenJacobsonAuthor
Bookbub: @ellenjacobsonauthor
Goodreads: Ellen Jacobson

ALSO BY ELLEN JACOBSON

The Mollie McGhie Sailing Mystery Series

Murder at the Marina (Book #1)
Bodies in the Boatyard (Book #2)
Poisoned by the Pier (Book #3)

CPSIA information can be obtained
at www.ICGtesting.com
Printed in the USA
BVHW072224070520
579403BV00001B/171